Praise

"In prose reminiscent of Fleur Jaeggy, *The Weak Spot* is a prismatic fable spiked with dozens of elegant revelations. Lucie Elven is an extremely promising new writer, one in touch with a greater, richer world that exists just below the surface of daily life."

—CATHERINE LACEY, author of
Pew and *The Answers*

"This eccentric, intensely observed book—full of dry humor and sturdy, elegant sentences—examines the slippery quality of the self in relation to others and the treacherous terrain of a world governed by manipulative men. Slightly gothic, vaguely old-world, and briskly contemporary, *The Weak Spot* is a singular work from a writer whose fiction I've long admired in the pages of *NOON*." —KATHRYN SCANLAN, author of
The Dominant Animal and *Aug 9—Fog*

"*The Weak Spot* is at once a charming and a gently profound novel, bringing to mind the elegant fabulism of Anne Serre and the grace-filled contemplativeness of Marilynne Robinson's *Housekeeping*. In

sentences that quietly astonish, Lucie Elven shows us how consciousness is shaped by landscape—by distance, light, and heat—and by radically opening ourselves, for better and for worse, to the aspirations and struggles of others. I know I will be returning to these pages again and again."   —MARY SOUTH, author of
You Will Never Be Forgotten

"Recalling the mood of Thomas Mann's *The Magic Mountain* and the aesthetic of a Dario Argento film, *The Weak Spot* is an evocative and intriguing novel. The thrill is in the prose—vivid, expansive, perfectly controlled. I love where Lucie Elven's sentences take me, and I adore this book."

—LAUREN AIMEE CURTIS, author of *Dolores*

"No word is wasted in Lucie Elven's whipsmart, elegiac debut. Every scene and image is vivid, cutting, and fluid, turning a peculiar mountain town into a wonderland of social insights and frictions. I knew I would be rereading *The Weak Spot* halfway during my first read—and a few pages into my second read. Elven is a master in the making."

—STEPHEN KEARSE, author of
In the Heat of the Light

THE WEAK SPOT

THE WEAK SPOT

LUCIE ELVEN

SOFT SKULL

NEW YORK

This is a work of fiction. All of the characters, organizations, and events portrayed in this novel are either products of the author's imagination or are used fictitiously.

ISBN: 978-1-59376-630-6

The Library of Congress Cataloging-in-Publication data is available.

Cover design & Soft Skull art direction by www.houseofthought.io
Book design by Wah-Ming Chang

Published by Soft Skull Press
1140 Broadway, Suite 704
New York, NY 10001
www.softskull.com

Printed in the United States of America
1 3 5 7 9 10 8 6 4 2

The phantoms of old were nothing other than people.

—CONTES DE LA LUNEIRA

THE WEAK SPOT

TELL ME ABOUT YOURSELF

The river moved quickly for such an unrushed place, curling around the base of the mountain, and at the crest of the town lay the golden side of a ruined abbey. A graveyard hung behind it, falling like a veil, two stones here, three there, others farther out dug into the rock face and jagging horizontally over the precipice, as if these sidelong burials had been a punishment for crimes.

Between the fir trees, long light-headed candles extending out of the steep incline, a passage had been carved out for the funicular. As it wound up its ancient, ticking mechanism, another car was coming down. We passed it in midair: a man chatting between two police officers and a woman standing by the driver. The light on them looked as solid as drapery. Even on such a blue day you could tell this sky had a knack for breaking into storms.

It was almost the time of my appointment with Mr. Malone when I arrived at the square with the pharmacy, a corner building so fastidiously closed it looked folded up. I stood in the middle of the plaza and turned in a full circle so that the houses rotated around me. Their second floors, which must have been the most desirable when the town was built, had shutters that were taller than those on any other floor. Above them in some cases were rows of square windows. I was thinking of my mother, for whom the third floor was the one that was tiring to get to, the floor that was a mystery, where any dangerous transformation might be happening to me—but I lost hold of her when I saw a dog trotting along the edge of the square. On its trail was a pair of shoes clacking loudly. It was Mr. Malone, with sunglasses on, whose face was bronzed and rich compared to his photograph on the Institute website. The dog, followed by Mr. Malone, took a corner into an alley off the square to the right of the pharmacy. The dog kept on to the end and Mr. Malone seemed to speed up, then stopped himself and watched it go. He reached into his jacket pocket, and unlocked a side door. A minute later, with a grinding, the shop's metal security grille cranked up.

Inside, wearing his white coat in front of the counter, Mr. Malone said, "Tell me about yourself." He followed up with questions like, "Why did you choose this town? When did you decide to train as a pharmacist?" I studied him. He was a large man of around fifty with an upper lip that dropped beautifully over his mouth. He looked unregulated and liable to weep yet also orderly, a wardrobe out of whose stuffed shelves coats and pillows would tumble if you opened the door without care.

It started there, at the beginning of our relationship, as soon as we met. Maybe it was because I'd seen him captivated by the stray dog, and I knew he was behaving differently now he was on his guard. I didn't tell him anything.

I didn't say that I had been near the town once on holiday when I was a child. My uncle had taken my mother and me on an interminable walk. We were on a path around the mountain but, as a joke, my uncle had lied, and told me we would be heading right up it. It was so foggy that we couldn't see where we were going. Every so often, he would point into the mist and announce, "Look! We're getting closer!" As we went, he had overpowered us with stories about a mythical monster local to the area that devoured humans neck-first, about a nun who had turned into a hillock, about the black sheep of the family, who had moved to a house nearby and pinned live flies under the needle of a gramophone so that they were slowly dismantled as he listened to Ravel. Later I learned that it was a part of the country that deviants ran away to in books, a place for murderers, thieves, and alcoholic former lawyers to lie low, a landscape full of abrupt drops, deep craters, boars, snakes, and wolves—a vast, sleeping boundary, a safe haven. At the end of my studies the town had appeared on the list of possible places to train. I wanted to see if I could measure up to this wildness. No one had quite said I couldn't, so I applied.

As for why I wanted to be pharmacist at all, that had no answer I was able to share with Mr. Malone.

While I responded in a deliberate monotone, guessing at what I might be expected to say, he interjected to check that he had understood a point or to ask about my private life. He told me to read my list of queries about the position aloud, rather than raise them one by one. He said he hoped that some link between my areas of uncertainty would lead us to an interesting topic of conversation. He asked if I knew the process for being approved by the pharmacy board after his two-month mentorship. He answered his own question: on his recommendation, I would interview over several hours with several more members of the Institute, after which two separate people had to approve me. Only then would I be allowed to run my own pharmacy.

Mr. Malone seemed to be snapping at me and cutting me off because he had already decided that I was not ready for the role. By all rights, I shouldn't have inserted myself into this thin-aired, close-knit mountain town—to me just a shapeless place where I felt something had been interrupted. My decision had been unrestrained, reckless. He mentioned that some people prefer to wait until they have children before training, then apologized for presuming. I explained to him that I had a strong instinct that this was what I wanted to do, and he said, yes, that came across, I clearly had profound emotions about it. I must have looked desperate as I explained I wasn't usually wrong when I acted on this sort of impulse. Something flickering entered his eyes. He asked me if I had any more questions, and I paused for as long as I thought would convey my ability to abide an uncomfortable situation, then said no. He disappeared down a forest-green corridor into a back office.

When I'm angry it is often a sign that I am trying to work something out, and this was surely happening now. I walked down the aisles and stared at a display of baby bottles, trying to draw a practical conclusion from this discouraging introduction. After all, he had struck a chord when he agreed about how important this opportunity was to me. He had created a deep trench of feeling in the room during our conversation.

But then Mr. Malone came back into the front of the shop.

He was briefly generous in explaining his

philosophy. He believed that a pharmacist's role was to enhance the locals' potential by listening skillfully. When he was a child, Mr. Malone said, he had told his parents he wanted to restore old cities. The town was forgetting itself year on year and the municipal authorities did such a careless job preserving its dignity and protecting the habits of the community that young women, especially, were moving away. When they visited their families, they had new singsong voices, as though they were on the radio, which seemed a betrayal to the older generation. The world was changing fast and people here always felt their efforts to keep up were a little off. They were trying to attract a new doctor, as the last one had retired to the city. Patients had to attend appointments over the internet, which was slow. Only that morning the mayor had been arrested. He was facing accusations of tax fraud. That was why our work at the pharmacy was particularly necessary.

Mr. Malone said that when the bell over the door rang, I was to experience customers' needs more urgently and their disappointments more keenly than my own. I was to ask them what they were hoping for, about their ambitions, and I was to remember all those details for the next time they came. Then his level of emotion went from overflowing to nothing. His face became a window with drawn curtains. He retired again to the back office.

IT'S SO HOT

I noticed that the windows didn't open. There were large jars and demijohns in front of them. The shop was empty of business, so after a couple of minutes I went to survey the area down the corridor with a cupboard, the kitchen, an upward staircase. On my way I ignored the back room with its open door— peripherally I could see Mr. Malone sitting at his desk, his feet up, loud shoes exchanged for slippers— employing an attitude I hoped was confidence. When I returned to the shop front, I found Elsa standing behind the counter. She hadn't known I was coming. We had to introduce ourselves. She explained that she helped organize the dispensing station of the pharmacy, pointing to a corner of the square room separated by a diaphanous blue curtain. It had just been the two of them, she said. She was pleased there would be someone new. She moved over and gestured apologetically at the space where she had been standing, and I stepped into it.

"It's so hot," I said. I could now see that a fan was positioned on a rafter in such a way that behind the counter conditions were infernal while the rest of the area stayed cool.

Elsa dipped down to a shelf under the counter and brought out a diagram she had made of the pharmacy, a plan to rearrange the shop so that working was more comfortable. "Now that you're here," she said firmly, "maybe we can suggest this to Mr. Malone." I realized she hadn't wanted to risk asking him by herself.

The drawing of the pharmacy took up most of the small sheet of paper, with greasy pencil lines and magnified proportions, as though it was the impression of an audience member looking up at a performance. The perspective hinted at the optical illusions created by the curved ceiling, the harlequin-tiled floors, and the old mirrors on the walls. Elsa had positioned the counter to one side so that the pharmacist stood next to the window rather than having her back to the corridor. Next to the box of the pharmacy she had sketched the tree on the square in intricate detail, its leaves like writing in a script I didn't understand, its bark swirling in black. The houses around it were just lines, as though she had suddenly given up.

The bell rang. It was an ageless man whom I recognized as the driver of the funicular I had seen coming down the mountain. Up close, his blue eyes seemed to be illuminated from inside his head, backlit, glittering. Raising his face up to the fan, he told Elsa and me that it was cooler in the pharmacy than outside. It was a relief to come out from behind the counter to bring a stool for him to sit on, and offer to make him some coffee.

As I walked down the corridor to the kitchen, I saw Mr. Malone popping a menthol for the throat and chest, his lips the color of his cheeks. He didn't seem to expect to be looking after customers. He appeared to have delegated his whole job to me already. His mentorship would be of the more oblique, unscientific kind, I thought, striking up the smallest ring of the stove. I supposed I should ask my uncle to send my suitcase, which I had left with him while I waited to hear if I was accepted. I put the Bialetti on the fire, then came back into the front. As I passed Mr. Malone's open door, he looked like he had forgotten who I was. He stared as if carried back in a trance.

ARMED WITH CLAWS

In the front, Mr. Funicular sat under the arch that framed the glass entrance, with its rounded panes set in rectangular doorframes. He was being jolly and garrulous, telling Elsa that his amateur dramatics were going well. For Mr. Funicular, it was the costumes. It had taken him decades to discover that making these was what he was ambitious about. He produced a sort of toy out of his pocket, an animal figurine fashioned out of fabrics of different provenance, gathered or fanning stiffly outward, about as tall as a fist altogether. Mr. Funicular said he had sewn it from some offcuts. It was meant to represent the local beast. He joked that it was so grotesque it might ward off illness.

Elsa took the doll from his hand and pinned it to the front of the counter. Despite the super-stition, I didn't protest. My reliance on tokens of intellectualism—symbols of abstract thinking and rationality—was one of the things my mother had found difficult about me. It was dangerous, exhaust-ing, infantile. During the years she had been ill she had stopped telling me what treatments she was trying, going on trips where she had poor reception. Then she had made a sudden recovery and become evangelical about alternative remedies. Our commu-nication was bad for a while, and over that time she had died in a car accident.

As Mr. Funicular began to talk he held his ears and rubbed them. Centuries ago there was, he told me, a spate of killings in the region. People started talking of a sullen and extraordinary beast that had settled here, which was eating girls alive. Through-out the whole country, the region became the land

of the beast. In that land, there was no more living. The lumberjacks didn't dare go into the forest.
Normal bustle was disturbed. The great fairs after
the harvest season were badly attended, and people
walked outside only in pairs and groups. The beast
could be hiding on the corner of the large path if you
passed at the wrong time, or in the brush, or behind
a juniper. Fear ruined the people who saw it. It cap-
sized some to the point where they never came back,
or else it led to illness. Mr. Funicular's eyes darted
beneath his little eyebrows, and his quick mouth
twisted.

People wondered if it would depopulate the region. It
seemed possible that it would kill enough people to scare
the rest away. Finally, the mysterious beast was tracked
and tormented so much that while it wasn't destroyed, it
was at least dislodged, and moved to another area.

As I had with my uncle, I asked what the beast
looked like.

Mr. Funicular seemed delighted and to know the
answer by heart. He told me that it was well stocked in
the tail department, armed with claws, too, otherwise

long and rather low. It knew how to flatten itself into the undergrowth. He said that the beast had tufts of raised hairs over its eyes. Its tail was four feet long, full, heavy, luxuriant, as fat as a limb. With its reddish fur, the black parting on its spine, and its thick, whipping tail, nobody could agree on what species it was. A monster, a hyena or a wolf crossed with god knows which leopard. The farmers at the time asked themselves if there was something else at play that went beyond nature.

I could smell burned rubber and leaped back to the kitchen. The Bialetti had exploded from the pressure of waiting, a coffee Rorschach blot all over the walls. Mr. Malone was sitting next door in the back office, doing the accounts. He had let this go on.

By the time I had cleaned up the walls and come back into the corridor, the office was empty. I tried to keep a deadpan face, but something must have transmitted, because when Elsa saw me she laughed and said that Mr. Malone had left for a meeting in the town hall. Mr. Funicular had gone also. The shadows were longer on the paving stones of the square.

THE WEAK SPOT

All our talking was not part of any sales strategy, Elsa explained. The customers came in one by one and disclosed as if at confession, and usually left without spending a cent.

A STRANGE VEGETABLE

Occasionally a tourist or a hiker walked in and Elsa marked up the price of a tube of toothpaste. But too few people passed through to make the pharmacy lucrative. The square was usually empty, and Elsa would stand at the entrance to say hello compulsively at even the barest glint of someone coming past, and dwell at length on the smallest of questions. When she said hello, the passerby said hello and added how are you, and when she responded, well, how are you, she always had another remark to add immediately after— oh, I'm not sure if you saw this or that. She would then hand the customer over to me. An alliance was forming between us. Sometimes we opened the doors up wide and set the stool down outside the pharmacy entrance, on the square. From there the customers talked and I listened, always staying behind my counter.

Mr. Malone's methods seemed fussy to me at first, but they were effective. The customers' stories would start with an update on their day, an anecdote that was often interrupted by the speakers' sudden shame that they were going in a direction that surprised them, revealing more than they anticipated. They came in with a fever, then told me about a fight. What was impressive was how each learned to plow on, to talk as if what was happening in their life was some sort of natural growth they just lived with, a strange vegetable that they could hold in their hands, weigh, and assess.

The customers also shared their impressions of Mr. Malone, referring to him by his forename, August. They speculated that he was frugal, refined, generous, hardworking, mischievous, saintly, and then looked at me for confirmation of their diagnoses. I felt that he wouldn't like me to respond, even to praise him behind his back: it spread him too thin. They all appeared to harbor a secret adoration, and whenever they commented on him they did so with affection. A number of the customers were regular visitors, and through our conversation would settle into an exploration of what they wanted from their lives.

It felt unbelievable to me that this was the work I had studied to do through years of university, yet it seemed to involve little scientific knowledge and mostly fragile intuition. Skeptical as the customers could be, they were always alive to anything I said that rang true to them, and I had to be clear and connect the first time I spoke, so that they would not be discouraged.

Not knowing how much faith to place in Mr. Malone's process, I eventually adopted it wholesale, so as not to think. I hoped that if I mastered it I would become accepted by the townspeople, and be understood in passing during my conversations with strangers. As much as I was there to serve the customers, I was also there to be understood. My uncle had liked to retell the walk we had taken, saying that

I had been dismissive and intimidating with the people in the nearby villages. Intimidating! To be called that by an uncle seemed obscene, a reversal of our ages. When I sent him my new address, he wrote back that he knew a few people in those parts, had been following a restaurateur from afar. He began to recall to me some salient facts about the difficulty of the country, encumbered as it was by mountains, cut through with torrents, with its embarrassment of forests. He mentioned the altitude of various peaks, the age of the abbey. He seemed eager to make contact, but I didn't reply.

HER TERRITORY

One afternoon at the end of my first week Elsa and I agreed that we would ask Mr. Malone about rearranging the pharmacy. It was so hot that day that to stop myself from fainting I had been planting my nails into my gums. I had to hold back from doing this when Mr. Malone swept into the front. But before I could bring up the heat behind the counter, Elsa launched into a personal story, to corner Mr. Malone into acknowledging that like the customers his workers, too, had overflowing inner worlds to tend to and develop.

Elsa's story was about her desire for a garden. It had been agreed at her mother's deathbed that in exchange for Elsa moving into one side of the house, the entire garden would go to Elsa's sister, Nelly, who had become terminally ill. Elsa had a mere patch of grass where the garage had been. It received no sun.

Her sister had been doing everything over the past few years to accumulate scraps of land here and there, and even a small wood, so that her territory, which bordered on Elsa's patch, was immense.

Elsa kept her voice low, though there was no one else in the pharmacy. She was speaking from the dispensing area, and Mr. Malone stood very still nearby, hovering on the threshold to the corridor. The question was: Should she wait for her sister's death before asking her nieces for the part of the garden behind her own house? Or should she ask a friend of hers to step in and buy the empty house on the other side of Nelly's garden and propose a path, a direct line from her friend's house to Elsa's, along which Elsa could plant flowers? She could offer to tend one of her sister's vegetable beds in exchange for this access.

Elsa's eyes tacked left and right as if she were plotting the route by which to climb out of the problem. It wasn't obvious to me whether Elsa deeply wanted a garden because of this family feud, or if the feud had centered, by misfortune, on the thing that she most wanted. What was evident was that Elsa was confused by her sister's ability to get her way.

Since Nelly's diagnosis, Elsa explained to Mr. Malone and me, her sister had become more caring; she noticed everything, hearing even the smallest voices, knowing what to say, showing a calm sense of direction and purpose. She had immediately left her job and gone about making amends to the family and friends she had sacrificed at its altar. With those reconciliations under her belt she had pried open the door to her desires. You have to tell people what you want in this life or they tell you, and sooner or later you get confused, Nelly had said to Elsa, over the garden wall.

Who was Elsa to begrudge her dying sister for getting exactly what she wanted? Elsa asked. It seemed to me that Elsa was angry with her sister precisely because she was going to die—that she was setting up a way in which she would benefit from such a painful certainty, so that she could tolerate it.

I wondered out loud why Elsa hadn't, up until

now, tried to get what she wanted herself. Because she spent her life protecting everyone else from disappointments, fending off other people's frustrations, Elsa said. She confessed to us that her own dream had always been that she would never have to explain what she wanted, that her experiences were etched into her appearance, and that should be enough for people to understand her.

But more and more often, she had found herself disappointed, and prone to revealing her complaints to someone indiscreet—the gossipy market seller, for example. She knew that this couldn't go on.

When Elsa finished talking, Mr. Malone straightened. With a bright air, he asked the elderly Helen Stole, who had just entered the shop on the arm of an attentive young man, if she had heard what Elsa had said.

Helen Stole had been a teacher to the whole town. She was always accompanied by some young person standing like a bodyguard, close enough to joke and bandy around a comment. Judgmental and capable, it seemed she could make something of anything that wasn't completely worthless. A pleasant terror radiated around her. She smiled at us expectantly one by one.

"Should Elsa wait until her sister dies before trying to get her hands on her garden?" Mr. Malone summarized, welcoming her into our conversation.

I looked over at Elsa. Her face hardened and her eyes slid away.

Helen Stole's gaze burned through us as she handed me her prescription. She left the shop without saying a word.

After this, the pharmacy stayed in its old configuration, with the counter in the heat. We never dared ask if we could change a thing. We didn't want to be cautious with Mr. Malone, but could no longer doubt that it was necessary.

IT WAS COMFORTING

There are different types of good behavior, I reasoned. Even when Mr. Malone was malicious, and humiliated us, it seemed to be for the greater good of making a customer laugh or feel trusted, or of prompting fruitful introspection in us. He had perfected a productive formality, and the art of abruptly closing a conversation was a part of that.

I wanted his tricks and shortcuts for myself. By being difficult to catch and maneuvering at speed, flashing in and out of rooms, Mr. Malone made being in his presence an intense and precarious experience. With his silent entrances and exits, I would go from

feeling that nobody was interested in my work to being uncomfortably aware that someone was sitting
somewhere just behind my field of vision, observing
me at my counter.

I had a low lip-line, according to Mr. Malone. My
hair was what he would describe as ashy, and it reminded him of his mother's. "It will never go gray," he
told me confidently.

In the afternoons he stepped out and left the
shop entirely in my care, but would hang back if a
customer was around to see him abandon his post.
He flipped on the glare of his attention like headlights, and listened, nodding, cocking his head. He
sat on a stool, positioning himself behind me as I
talked to a man with a dappled, freckled complex-
ion and a paunch. The man described how since
his wife had become pregnant he was putting on
weight, sleeping badly, and getting nosebleeds. He
said he wasn't sure he wanted a baby. Seeing him
in distress was intolerable and I rushed to patch
things up. A thought occurred to me, or maybe it
was a feeling, or at least the thought could not have
existed without me choosing not to turn the feeling

away. Maybe it wasn't that he didn't want a baby but that he didn't feel he was capable enough to be a father, I assured him.

After the man left, Mr. Malone said that my method had been a damning failure, a missed opportunity. I had told the man what he was like, he continued, which the man hadn't appreciated. As a result, the man's narrative hadn't traveled enough, our conversation had ended before anything could happen. I surveyed Mr. Malone as I digested this, the way he made his mouth into a tunnel as he criticized me, how he loomed slightly, and spoke as if from the back of his head, like someone reciting from memory. I felt a paralyzed calm set in. It was comforting to draw a line through the interaction and never try the same tactic again.

Since the incident with the garden anecdote, Elsa had started to move differently, out of fear. Banks of boxes fell over in the dispensing area when Mr. Malone was in the room with us. I could see her shoulder tipping or her head dropping, see her inability to anticipate what her body was meant to be doing.

I began to employ Mr. Malone's turns of phrase,

and to open my eyes, as he did, at the outer edges, as though I had just emerged from a cold wind, to show I was alert and listening. I tried to embody a youthful energy I had almost forgotten. I practiced this in the morning and evening while crossing the series of streets where men wore baseball caps and greased their hair and called out to me between the pharmacy and my narrow house.

ANOTHER LEVEL

I lived on the edge of a row of terraces that sliced into the pavement like a diamond or a knife. It was the open end of the town reaching toward the valley, another fold in the universe that was differently lit, half-auburn, half-blue. The notable old homes in the center, with their faded embellishments, gave way to more angular, alive ones, with clouds of white steam spouting from the walls, tubes protruding out of windows, water bubbling up from grates, and passages that opened like throats under stacks of windows. My house's windows and doors were long and unevenly arranged. Before her death, it had belonged

LUCIE ELVEN

to a painter who had used it to get away from her demanding life in the capital, and no one could understand what chain of connections had enabled Mr. Malone to secure it for me. Inside, the walls were midnight blue and jewel green.

When I had rushed to the town and moved into the empty house, I bought chairs on the internet, surprised by their quick shipping and apparent value for money. When they arrived they turned out to be made for a dollhouse, no more than a thumb high. I returned them with apologies and compliments to their maker, but not before I had arranged them in each of the rooms, by the kitchen table, at the foot of my bed, next to the bathroom sink, to see them dwarfed by the surroundings. I found this very funny and had to sit down on the side of the tub. In the mirror I could see telltale silver hairs, somehow longer than the others, streaking my crown. It occurred to me that there was something reassuring about the obviously dangerous Mr. Malone to someone like me who worried all the time. From a young age I'd had the permanent feeling of having narrowly escaped a bad crowd.

My family were compulsively helpful people, and

34

in their acute helpfulness they often sacrificed safety and softness for the sense that they were giving and saving and showing resilience. As a child, I had often listed each of the eventualities I feared, warding them off before bed in reams of fervent legalese. Then I had ordered my dreams, as if from a waiter in a restaurant. I had at that age been trying to avoid a recurring nightmare that a wolf would ring the doorbell of my house and be let into the kitchen by my parents. My parents and the wolf would hunch over the table together, extending their nails on the wax cloth, and agree on the rules of a game.

The aim was to be the first to reach the top of the house, my room on the third floor. If I heard the wolf's steps and hid, he would get ahead of me, and he would scan every object carefully on the way back down until he found me. Several times, hearing him approach, I climbed into a cavernous chest full of fabrics in an in-between room where there was a door that had once led to a secret passageway from the cellar, before it was cemented in. When I hid myself in there, the lid of the chest inevitably opened on a pair of yellow eyes.

One night a safe room materialized, a red room on another level, whose entrance was buried in one of a row of cupboards in a part of the house I didn't often visit. In real life this room didn't exist.

THE SLIGHTEST IMBALANCE

I had been at the town only a few weeks when the first storm broke. A rock of ice hit the window by my head and the glass cracked apart, sending in hailstones. I had been sleeping on my front with only my feet enclosed by the sheet, always in the same splayed position, and got out of the way by forming a ball on the dry side of the bed as thunder followed lightning. The next morning when I left for work, it was summer again. Water vapors were rising from the forests. The air had a warm, furtive smell. Some of the clouds looked like cracked earth, some like they were cultivating produce and had been tilled in irregular lines.

A dramatic wisp rode like smoke past this layer, a superficial desperado. I saw Helen Stole through her kitchen window, eating a peach over the sink. She called me over to say hello properly, then moved into the easy chair next to her front door. A rope of blue steam drummed out of the window, catching the light. She asked me how I had found the town, and I told her about the walk with my uncle and admitted my hasty decision. She said that sometimes choices that had been made thoughtlessly and fast were better than the ones we focused on too hard. I asked her about herself, and she mentioned local associations she had a role in, boards she sat on, groups with which she planned and campaigned. She told me she ran a craft society and a modest bodybuilding class. "And how's August Malone treating you?" she asked, making the name stand up with a touch of something that was not quite irony, not quite affection.

It was important to me that I describe my last few weeks as they had happened, and yet I knew that if I described them exactly I would be in trouble with Mr. Malone. I liked the way he was so methodical, I told her. On the armrest her fist was a rectangle, and her finger twitched. I said that maybe he had seen something in me. I leaned forward and explained I sometimes had this feeling that with the right method I could transform one thing into another. She looked disapproving but even that made me feel good. I glanced down at the ground, where branches lay spread across the asphalt like snakes that didn't writhe, their leaves still on them, and turned back to Helen, who was beckoning to me confidentially. She described a number of symptoms she was experiencing. I recommended something gentle.

But my sense of magician-like importance didn't last. As it grew hotter, my sentences got shorter. By the end of one month, I decided I had no ego left. I could be swayed by this or that person, because no part of me resisted being disturbed. Like a contortionist threading her fillet of a body through her arms, I automatically climbed into the customers' perspective. I doubted myself constantly, wondering what I had forgotten, and what I had accepted as truth by repeating it. I felt that each of the townspeople lived inside my body and rocked me from side to side, so that I could no longer judge whose side to privately take in an argument between neighbors, or who was hopeful, who exaggerated, who was insightful, who was bureaucratic, who was merely anxious. It was as if I employed my mouth to make the shapes of the lyrics of whatever song was filling the high walls, sonorous, resounding, vibrato. My opinion of an event could change several times in a day.

I was sure the customers thought of me as boring—why else did I ask them about their lives, week after week?—so I was self-deprecating, and soon learned that this was the right way to behave. When the market seller arrived mumbling something about the colorful clothes I wore, I told him, "I'm trying to find myself!" and at this Mr. Malone laughed appreciatively from the back room.

Despite having little sense of what would happen when I parted my lips to talk, sometimes my urge to hold forth about myself could turn physical, like a desire to eat, as if my story could paint the room or fill it. I knew that the slightest imbalance to my system would send me over the edge, saying too much, and that in order to mitigate myself I shouldn't touch caffeine, or join the customers in a glass of the liqueur we kept in the kitchen and that I had been told to offer them on some evenings. Instead I drank decaf, which had a damp-rag aroma.

Nothing was more unbearable for me than kind attention. So when Helen Stole sent a note over with Mr. Funicular to let me know that the Senokot I'd recommended to her had improved her life, I couldn't look at the piece of paper directly. When Mr. Funicular cajoled that I was working too hard, I snapped the inventory shut and drew away. But when I asked the customers my own questions, they responded with pleasure. The more abstinent I seemed, the more they talked.

Sometimes it worried me to think about what Mr. Malone did with the information I was stacking up within earshot, as he sat in the room down the corridor behind me, doing the accounts. I wondered if the customers would have told him so openly about their affairs and debts, or started on their trivial worries, like whether a cat was still nursing her kitten, or how to air their houses at night when there was a loud dispute going on next door, banal beginnings that led to something else that had been numbed. But if the days were hot, too hot even to come out from my hiding place behind the counter and sweat coarsely in front of the clientele, I just wanted to relax, forget about myself, and hear a new explosive confidence.

CORD

I was easy to derail. I derailed myself on my own. Unless I was busy, I was distracted by daydreams.

The hairdresser was called Bianca, a niece of Elsa's. She wore a long plait. She was one of the few people I could talk to because she didn't seem particularly interested in holding on to anything I said, or in unburdening herself to me in return. One night, as she applied ash brown dye through my hair—I wanted to preserve the favorable position I was given for being young—I fantasized about being the perfect mannequin. She moved my head with both hands straight-fingered and held it, tilted diagonally. It was a different kind of touch, a touch at once formal and intimate. I had thought I was like a statue, a symbol of stillness, of the possibility of calm, avoiding stressful movement, delaying gratification. She told me about a family wedding she was going to.

Alone in the pharmacy the next day I imagined the people drinking paper cups of coffee outside the church all day and, in the late afternoon, Elsa and Nelly sitting on the high stools in the bar, the entrance of which was marked by a dark lantern. There were two bars in the town—this one, in the dip in the land by the funicular, and another Mr. Malone had mentioned once at the top by the abbey. The sisters conversed about the party in a collaborative rhythm, with the intensity of fury. Everyone was murmuring in gentle, heartfelt, velvety tones, which made Elsa and Nelly want to bulldoze through. They rehashed stories that hung around in their family like ancestors clinging on and exerting pressure. Nelly was putting words into mouths. Elsa allowed herself to accept Nelly's versions of stories, though she knew they were incomplete, and to repeat them. Maybe she expected gratitude from her sister, or wanted to set aside their rivalry for a day. "We're biased," Nelly informed her.

Elsa changed the subject and said that when she looked through the photographer's images of the wedding she had been disappointed that she wasn't in more of them, to see an event through the lens of something official, the future, and be left out. She looked in the mirror behind the bar. As she got older there seemed to be an increasing separation between her hair and her face. She was aware that her shoulders looked theatrically narrow. She noticed that as an unmarried woman she had been asked to help prepare the large spread of food that was laid out beside them.

Elsa caught a man's eye in the reflection of the wall of the bar. He reminded her of someone, but maybe he was an old friend's father. One of her problems was that she thought she recognized people everywhere. You couldn't introduce her to a situation without her trying to convince you she had locked eyes with someone she recognized, trying to form a link, perhaps, to explain how she had gone from A to B in life.

Elsa continued to chat. The man looked over

again, and he raised his glass at her. She raised hers back and ducked behind a pillar. Finally she asked Nelly, who knew everyone, and Nelly identified him as the friend's father Elsa thought she'd recognized. Elsa expressed her love for Nelly offhandedly, like a rejection of herself.

"Who's going to eat all of this?" said their boring aunt, coming over and tasting the panna cotta. And soon there was no panna cotta left.

Bianca left the bar carefully. She seemed so nervous and overcasual as she tried to exit in an agreeable way that Elsa and Nelly noticed her. Bianca walked back into the empty church until she reached a triangle of sun at the front. She felt the light open up her face. A cord was tied to the side of the pew, a shining rope. Bianca whipped it up and around so that it snaked and jumped. The sisters found her there. They tried to jump to the movement of the rope in time. There was music outside but it didn't align to the rhythm of the rope.

After I articulated this sort of reverie I felt a sense of revulsion.

COMPULSIVE FABRICATOR

On the first of September, Mr. Malone let us know he was ill, a situation that seemed impossible. The alley door was locked, as was the door to the back room next to the pharmacy kitchen. Unaware, the customers still asked after him courteously, as though he were still sitting just out of reach in his office. Their love seemed to be a side effect of him treating them as though he could see their souls. That must have been why we all revered him so much, why we looked into his house as we walked past, why we felt like we owned him.

In the afternoon, I admitted he was absent. The

customers took this opportunity to lean forward across the counter and wonder what it was like to work with him. They asked the way you might ask about someone's visit to an exotic country, and I replied as though reporting back about a time abroad. I soon regretted letting this start. I was not sure if I was portraying my new life correctly. I listlessly started a sequence of sentences until I came upon something surprising. I was hoping that, like in a ritual, my descriptions would become real, and that my days in the pharmacy would assume a different form as a result.

I pretended not to hear when one customer, an accountant who seemed to be quite new to the town, mentioned Mr. Malone's name. He carried on asking. He was anxious, slight, and his speech was marked by swallowed words and deep breaths. On learning he was gone, the accountant asked for Mr. Malone's address, so that he could visit his sickbed. "Imagine August," the accountant said in an overfamiliar tone, "lying awake in the dark watching the sunlight coming in around the curtains." His voice sounded like a shameful sob. Used to giving all that I could, I passed the information on.

When the accountant returned, he talked almost drunkenly, as though he didn't quite trust me but couldn't help confiding in me anyway. He announced that Mr. Malone was not at all ill. After years of deliberation, Mr. Malone was absent from work because he had decided to adopt a dog. He had been slow to make the decision. Between the idea and its execution, Mr. Malone had told the accountant, he had seen the town empty around him, whole families erased, and train lines that had been the arteries of the local area close or stations destaffed and fitted with ticket machines.

He was all the better for it, reported the customers who came across him in the valley, walking avenues of old oaks.

We received regular news of Mr. Malone from them now, especially the accountant, who was gaining in confidence and had taken to laying his briefcase down on the counter every morning, Elsa always left at half past ten, when we expected him in the pharmacy, and I would make an excuse to call her back. At around noon like clockwork his assistant, Lydia, would come in looking harried, to retrieve him.

The accountant brought with him a series of con-
fusions. He dropped into conversation things about
Mr. Malone that we hadn't realized, and made a point
of reminding me that I didn't have all the information
that was significant.

He told us he had been to dinner with Mr. Malone
and some of his friends—the gossipy market seller, a
historian—in the restaurant of the town's hotel. "The
food!" He went over the menu as if running through
a burning drama, his hands making circular motions.
"There was every kind of mushroom, game, boar." His
eyes had a faraway sheen. "The restaurateur is a monk
who has left the order. And while I was unfortunately
not hungry," he added, "I could appreciate the quality of the place." As he talked, he picked through the
papers on the counter. I wondered if Mr. Malone had
asked him to check up on us.

All the walking had given Mr. Malone time to
think, the accountant suggested. He kept mentioning
Mr. Malone's plan, which I didn't know about. Had
something led Mr. Malone to exclude Elsa and me? I
had started to accept the principle that he always had
a reason behind his actions.

I hadn't been paid for the month, and money hung over me all the time. I went to sleep adding and subtracting amounts from my bank balance, counting the expenses I had run up and the sums I had been promised.

The heat behind the counter was atrocious. Elsa and I had renamed parts of the room. We referred to the section for embarrassing conditions as the middle bridge, the shelves lining the walls were the skyscrapers, the dispensing area the sea. We called the counter the oven. Sometimes I suffered so much that I wanted to undress, as if the solution to discomfort were degradation. Elsa suggested we take advantage of Mr. Malone's absence to rearrange the shop, but the accountant was discouraging. I batted his hand away from Elsa's sketch. He seemed to think he was entitled to give his opinion, that he had to gainsay Elsa and me. I felt that it was a lesson he had learned from Mr. Malone. Perhaps something critical had been said over dinner at the hotel restaurant. Maybe the plan was for the pharmacy to close, or maybe the accountant was just a compulsive fabricator. Clearly, somewhere along the line we were being gulled. I must have forgotten something, I thought, and I spent days raking over every interaction I could summon back for a clue, trying to work out where the blanks began and ended. "This is possibly the best . . ." I remembered once stating. "This is usually effective . . ."

Two weeks later, listless and sedated by the heat, I succumbed and made real coffee. That day we finally heard Mr. Malone click open the door of the back room. Now that he was back, there was an aura of crisis, although we pretended there was not. I sensed him keeping me within earshot. He called to me as I listened to the accountant—and there he was with a grin, sitting in the back room, while I made more pots of coffee to help his pharmacy run smoothly, because it takes painful effort to be rude when it's appropriate. I got on my knees and began stacking away the papers and maps that were all over the floor in there, thinking it strange that they should already be so disordered when Mr. Malone had been back only an hour, and dimly conscious that he might have emptied the filing cabinets deliberately, work I was undoing. I was so disappointed in myself as he insisted, with a smile, that it wasn't necessary. It felt automatic, although I had never cleared up his papers before, and I hoped he would understand it was something I was doing out of pride, and not because I wanted to show any allegiance to him. But if anything the tidying, with him as a witness, made me doubt that there was any comfort to be found in gestures of enormous capability when I was constitutionally unable to defend myself.

"What is it that you're interested in?" Mr. Malone asked. "You're not interested in politics."

I said nothing.

He patted the desk before him, experimenting with applying pressure.

"I'm bringing in someone else to help me with my work," he said finally. He said he was telling me directly as a courtesy.

I didn't reply, or give him any reaction to savor. I could see him sitting back onto the desk and looking down at me.

He told me that Helen Stole was in a critical condition. Her mouth, lips, tongue, and throat had all swollen up after taking the Senokot.

I had the sensation of falling. I didn't know what would happen next, if a phone would ring somewhere, if I would be conveyed down the funicular arm in arm with two policemen. What did he want me to say? It must have been my fault, and I started to describe other mistakes I felt I might have made. "Go on," he said, until I had told them all. My confessions knotted around me like ivy, and I could tell from his expression that Mr. Malone believed that we observe people best from an angle: when they are in a rage, when they are our parents, or when, panicking, they have lost control of themselves.

CHAIR WITH A BUSTED SEAT

That evening I backed away from the pharmacy, walking farther to the top of the town than I ever had, following each street to its cooler end, gaining height. A flood of extreme awareness had come over me, an urgent sense there must have been an absence of attention beforehand, and that it had been lying dormant over the time I avoided being alone and absorbed talkative people. I needed to feel my muscles and nerves were real by making them ache. The short conversation I'd had with Helen the day after the storm stretched out in front of me, pulled out of all proportion until it seemed threadbare, like a net.

In my pocket I had the piece of paper I'd walked out of Mr. Malone's back office with. On it I had written the name of the hospital she was in, which I had thought I would rush to before I had realized that in the valley the trains to the city were so rare that I couldn't possibly leave without having planned the trip. Turning the sheet over in my hands, I found a list of names on the back with August Malone's at the top. The handwriting started off in gold and then became pencil as different people had added to it. A local historian, the gossipy market seller, the accountant . . . I kept climbing. I must have forgotten to check a detail of Helen Stole's medical history. All these days treating the events in people's lives as if they were as momentous as illnesses had made me forget about her frail body. I felt a broadening as I came up the hill, stopped when I saw something fantastical: the abbey dangling over the line of the houses. Under it would be the graves of other Augusts, other Helens, the tombs of entire families, buried together.

I looked into the dark landscape. I remembered how reluctant I had been to go on the walk with my uncle and mother, and my uncle trying to convince me, showing me the route up the mountain on the map. That summer, my mother had been ill but had not yet told my uncle. He had cried at first when I turned the idea down. "Come on, come on," my mother had said. Then we had walked, along a river lined with trees like mottled necks, working our bodies to exhaustion.

A star dived across the sky.

In the crevasse off the side of the mountain, plants climbed while rocks fell. What I liked about Helen Stole, I thought, was that she never made me feel like she couldn't understand me although she was of a different generation, or that I needed to speak up to be heard, although I was from another part of the country.

In the dusk, the abbey looked ragged, moth-eaten, a molting crow. I had a vision of facing the town in disgrace, former students of Helen's setting off firecrackers, banging pans, honking their motorbike horns outside my window all through the night, and in the morning myself, raised up on a chair with a busted seat, wriggling as pieces of cane splayed around me, being paraded through the streets to the funicular, leaving with no hope of recommendation to the Institute, and going home. I stood on the verge of the drop with my hands over my mouth. My hands had a strong smell.

I pushed open the door of the abbey and pretended to admire the altarpiece, with its characters tipping their heads, variously devotional, blinded, knocked out by the grace of god. They looked as though they had been drinking. In the center of the large frame was somebody who seemed to be having his tooth pulled out. Another painting was by a member of the school of tenebrism, and almost nothing was visible. There was a statue of a local saint, and below it a sign explaining that a hat was put on his head when the harvest was good. He was wearing the hat.

A nun arrived at my shoulder. She pointed at a square of glass that had been laid in place of a tile. There was an angled mirror down there, reflecting the saint's coffin, short and thin. The nun then pointed beyond the choir to a second room, more like a hall, and obediently I went over. The chill here was sweet and penetrating, as if I were walking by a river. The air had a tang of sherry. A sign saying DO NOT

ENTER hung off a lime-green curtain, and in the center of the space stood dilapidated nativities, statues, heads of St. John the Baptist, icons of pink popes, and turquoise-clad dolls dressed up as the holy family. The nun appeared in the door, seeming to be lurking in wait for me to leave, to give up. I scowled, unable to get outside myself. Who was I looking at these for? Was it for her? God to me was just a friend of a friend, seemingly benevolent with the potential to be untrustworthy. I paused before each artifact. She left through the door behind the curtain.

That night, in my bed, I wanted to paper over my guilt by going to sleep, to use sleep like a lie to forget the scene outside Helen's house, her enlarging kindness, my tall, spidery confidence. But I had started to feel as though I wouldn't wake up, was scared I would disappear.

THE WEATHER WAS TURNING

At the end of September, I was surprised to receive a letter from the Institute with an invitation to interview in the nearest city. The pharmacy doors were open, the breeze constant, and all the birds were calling to one another, making preparations for migration.

I walked out onto the square. In the distance, along from rockier terrain, the line of the plateau was straight, pencil-drawn, and would sometimes fall and continue farther down. That line traversed the whole of my time in the town—the path zigzagging along the ridge I had traced in my mind, with views, expansive, on either side.

A few days earlier, Mr. Malone's new assistant, Annie Milk, had arrived, wearing a skirt that had traveled well, seemed to have been carefully folded, and made her look neat and elongated. I could see why Mr. Malone liked her—she didn't draw attention to herself. It must have helped, also, that she was Helen Stole's granddaughter. Elsa had tried the usual routine when she came into the shop, asking her about herself, while I had retreated to the kitchen out of shame. Without me seeing how it was done, Annie Milk had made it to the back room without sharing anything, and closed the door. That day I was finally paid.

I didn't ask Mr. Malone why he had recommended me to the Institute after I had put Helen Stole in a critical condition—he seemed more concerned with meeting a series of landlords and surveyors, who I would send down the corridor to his office. Mr. Funicular speculated, in the way that customers did, that Mr. Malone was far more philosophical than I gave him credit for. I was not sure who else in the town knew about my negligence, and hoped it was not what the market seller was talking about when he scuttled around collecting rumors and having tea with neighbors. More for myself than for them, I assured Elsa and Mr. Funicular that I would visit Helen Stole in the hospital after my interview in a month.

The weather was turning. On the square, the wind stirred through the leaves of the tree like a reader shifting in bed. A mouse scratched its magnum opus in the walls. Mr. Funicular wrapped himself up to go back outside and Elsa laughed. He was beautiful in a way that the word didn't cover: the silhouette of a chess piece, a drop of molten metal, in his bowler hat and a pregnant belly where he was carrying a parcel underneath his long black overcoat.

I AM NOW CLOSING THE DOORS

When the customers came into the pharmacy look-ing distracted, I pictured what they had been doing a few hours before.

I am now closing the doors, said the accountant to his embattled assistant, Lydia. She played along, drawing the curtains and switching on the angle-poise lamp, then leaving his office with a look over her shoulder.

Once the doors were shut, the accountant lay back in his chair and dangled his legs about. He placed his calves up on the desk. He was sleepy. He knew that out-side that door, Lydia was alphabetizing all his folders.

That night, he was celebrating his friend the historian's latest success. Lydia had received a box marked FRAGILE, a present sealed with green-tinted cellotape.

The accountant knew the rest of the crowd that would be at the hotel restaurant. It was a crowd in which it was important to catch signals, to react quickly, to play the attention-grabbing game well, where people were alternately vying for your time and ignoring you.

The man he adored would be there too, reasonable, calm, talking about the facts he had learned about what had to be done in order to measure the value of land, and so on. The accountant hoped Mr. Malone would come by himself this time. He wanted to become closer to him, to be his associate. When the accountant met Mr. Malone with Annie Milk, he felt as though he were at the foot of a huge statue.

Once, when he had been drinking and someone asked him about his relationship with the pharmacist, the accountant had laughed harshly and raised his forearms in front of him, turning his hands like marionettes. "What is it you're suggesting?" he said, flashing his eyes insanely. Three days later, he still had not recovered from the stress of that conversation.

Lydia had hidden the clock behind some books on a towering shelf, from where it boomed out the time.

Some evenings the anxiety came over him like ecstasy.

STANDARDS

Over the month of October, the temperature dropped. Elsa told me, as I was going to the city, that it was possible to reach the station on foot. She described a route along a series of crumbling walls, gates into large vegetable gardens with wells and fruit trees, and a path that took you past a little concrete bridge to an island of river rocks covered in tall weeds. The water was wide between here and the other bank, and often rushing. You could sit in it and be two hundred meters downstream by the time you had extricated yourself.

When I arrived at the concrete bridge on the

Monday of my interview, the river was shallow and trapped in ice. Stones humped all along its width. Twigs stuck up like microphones from the oily mud. Trees split and jutted haphazardly out of the verge, and I wondered if these could be the thick, neck-like ones I remembered. From here, the town looked worrying and aggressive. I walked along to the road before taking the sharp right to the old station building.

The members of the Institute had asked me to meet them at a restaurant they had picked. There was a flurry of snow when they arrived, their bodies and their scarves bundled into their long coats, heading through the open door and saying hello to one another as they milled about the round tables, inside and outside the lit doorway.

These Institute people were momentous, craggy intellectuals, city people. All of them specialized in one area of medicine or another. All were very impressive alone and more so as a team because of their seeming ability to work together, as a machine, despite their considerable individual charisma. They were poised and talked as though held and handled by different points of view. Each was in the center of their own galaxy of ego, with their colleagues spinning around them. They seemed the kind of people who tuned in to a frequency of deep focus, solved a problem, then tuned out, moved on, and forgot, who floated so as not to have heavy depressions.

We took a large table that stretched the whole length of a wall and they asked the waiter for wine. One member told me that Mr. Malone was one of the few people who scared him, and he didn't know why. I couldn't tell if this was supposed to be a compliment. The waiter came with the wine and we ordered food.

"Shall we begin?" asked one woman.

"Yes," I agreed.

Later, I walked around a department store, taking the jackets by the lapels, giving them a straighten. Helen Stole seemed too significant to approach.

Slowly I gravitated in the direction of the hospital. The coffee vending machine in the waiting room looked as though she had not moved since the 1970s. She was upright, eloquent, disarming, engaged, and slightly impatient. Her lights were on, they dreamed and slid and railed. They gave her a halo.

Helen Stole's bed was on the top floor, with a

panoramic view of the water and the great black ca-
thedral from its long, wide window. She joked, "We
meet again," as I came into the room, which looked
like a dentist's office, with three reclining beds, two of
which were occupied by her and a businessman who
was reading his laptop, sitting upright in his gown, his
suit folded over the chair next to the bed. I wouldn't
have been able to describe Helen before, but now that
she was in front of me I knew the color of her flesh
had changed, her weight slightly reduced, and a plastic
wristband added since I last saw her.

She said to me, in her quiet and gravelly voice,
which seemed always to be in a rhythm, that she
thought the businessman, who had been sending
people to the hospital shop all day to buy him cig-
arettes, needed closer attention than he was being
given, but our conversation was interrupted by the
nurse coming in to take blood tests. She kept telling Helen how good she was being. At the last test,
the nurse tilted her chin up. The businessman and
I looked on in polite consternation. The vein had
stopped giving blood.

Something seemed to be happening around the

businessman now. His bed was being cranked down and another nurse was bending over his side table. I turned away. Buttoned up in my winter coat, I could almost feel the thin ache from the needle, my body seemed oddly uniform, warm and intensely indoors, and I wasn't keen on waiting around while the nurse tried again with the vein. "I'm feeling faint," I explained apologetically. Then my vision went. When I came to, they were handing me a cold cup of water and laying me on the third bed, telling me to close my eyes, yawn open my lips a little. I told them how embarrassing this was, that I used to faint all the time when I was younger, even though I wasn't exactly embarrassed and was hoping to bring in the businessman, who I was now sure had fainted first. When he made no admission of his own, I inquired if fainting was contagious, and the nurse told me that it was; seeing someone pass out can tip you over. They'd noticed it before.

The nurses left the room, and I asked Helen Stole what had happened. She said she had been walking home on Mr. Malone's arm, counseling him on one of his schemes, when she had felt a sting in her throat, like a bee's, which was followed by a hardening. He walked her to the door, and as she arrived on the step she discovered that she couldn't breathe properly. He called a helicopter ambulance. She said that her throat had always been her weak spot, that from a young age she had caught colds, lost her voice, had swellings, allergic reactions, tonsillitis, glandular fever, and even once a cyst on her voice box that had declared itself after a period when she had been working too hard. She wasn't surprised it had brought her down again.

I checked with her that the swelling and choking happened long after she had stopped taking the Senokot, and she said they had. She began to tell me about spending the winter in the city each year, how she wouldn't be back in the town until May when the weather became milder, and was sad not to be with her granddaughter Annie, while she was staying in her house there. I felt exhaustion set in. My fear that I had hurt her slowly loosened, except it didn't exactly lift, and in fact I seemed heavier. I was still sweaty, and my voice sounded rehearsed, sunken and slow, like something being dragged along the bottom of the frozen river.

At the station, lines of slow people sped up at the threshold of the escalator. A girl sneezed, and someone down the platform said, "Bless you." A man who was clipping his nails as he waited offered his seat to a stylish woman. In the carriage, another person asked me if she was on the right train, while somebody else complained about the speed with which the doors closed. The station attendant checked his watch ostentatiously, looked around, unfastened a steel box, slammed it shut, and we began taking in great volumes of land.

I gathered myself up, made a show of observing the carriage. There is a window of time in which, like blood coagulating, the collective atmosphere of a group is formed. I opened the sides of my eyes, raised my eyebrows at the people I walked past, swiveled sharply into a seat. As I imposed my standards on the teenagers on their phones, the reception was positive. After all, people who behave decadently and outrageously, who try to cause a stir, like to be remarked upon, for someone to cough or to repeat loudly what they say.

Life is short. When I acted like Mr. Malone, it gave me a feeling of magical control.

A REMINDER

Back between the four walls of the pharmacy, Mr. Malone told me the Institute had approved my candidacy. He said they had given a big shrug, in case I thought they had shown enthusiasm. The timing was perfect because he was planning on taking a sabbatical. I could have the pharmacy. I thanked him but he looked pained. "Please stop thanking me," he said. The fact he had let me feel guilty about Helen Stole was too painful to pass on.

Now that he had given me his approval, everyone warmed to me and introduced me to their babies, who were the products of matches Mr. Malone had made. I found myself developing a wavering voice, showing myself to be affected. I tipped my head back and parted my mouth in sympathy when I felt it was right, looking at the customers with wonder, as if I couldn't believe they fit into my frame of vision. I continued Mr. Malone's habit of being proud of everyone, tart, quick. But I also noticed people treating me with slight fear, opening doors for me, taking me too seriously, deferring to me to when I was wrong.

Mr. Malone even asked me what we should do to make the shop more appealing. Despite his sabbatical he was still coming in every morning, organizing his papers with Annie Milk, who showed little interest in pharmacy. He couldn't seem to let the place go. I opened the question up to the others. It was cooler now so there was no need to bring up the rearrangement, and Elsa seemed wary of answering with her drawing. To fill a long silence, Annie Milk, as a joke, suggested a water feature. Mr. Malone walked into the middle of the room. "Here?" he asked. He bent over and shucked a loose tile out of the floor, as if starting the project of digging. He paused, looked from left to right, and took the tile with him back into his office. It never came back, a reminder of Annie Milk's frivolity.

Now that I was in charge, I observed that Elsa derived an increasing amount of comfort from talking, whether it was setting a record straight or setting it more askew, making sure that I knew the world was strange and that people behaved irrationally. She would seize the reins of a conversation to start a sad story, and you knew it would be endless. "Do you remember," she would say to whoever walked in, "the summer when my mother had her fall?" It was after the sisters had gone on a long walk with her, and her mother had set off ahead because she didn't want to slow the two of them down. And she had been carrying three liters of water in her bag because she was carrying the water for everyone. But of course she didn't let herself drink, because she wanted there to be enough for them all. And then she had gotten lost, and no one else had water, so she was carrying all the water and not drinking any and no one else was drinking either. And the next day, she had collapsed in her orchard and damaged her skull. Elsa sped up and swelled in volume and emotion at the end of a sentence, anticipating being interrupted.

And Elsa's sister, Nelly, when she happened to be in the shop, was the same. "No," she would counter, their mother hadn't fallen after the walk. It was several days later, and she called Nelly into the basement, after Elsa and her friend had gone to the city and left her there alone. And then Elsa and her friend drove home and saw the helicopter over the town, and they were both laughing, wondering what was going on.

Elsa's sister was very confident about her memory, and Elsa was defensive.

Elsa said, "I was there."

"Was August there too? Yes, he was there, wearing some new shoes."

"No, no, it was just me."

"Who was the other man with you, then?"

"There wasn't one."

Nelly looked at Elsa disbelievingly.

When we were alone, I observed that Elsa was most relaxed when we talked over each other at high speed, each starting a sentence before the other finished. She was quick with jokes, teasing to bring me closer,

and sometimes I didn't have time to think about what
was going on inside her head at all—I felt I had to cut
through her patter and interrupt at any cost. When
she was gone I felt fondness, but when she was there
it was a case of trying to get through. She complained
of hating Annie Milk. I didn't like that I could predict
her thoughts because, after all the days working together, they were exactly the same as mine. I decided
to make some distance.

If I had a criticism to make of Elsa I would describe something the accountant had done, affixing
Elsa's own bad behavior to him, so that Elsa would
feel like she had come close to, but just gotten away
with, upsetting me.

I involved myself very little during the day, and at
the end of it check whether there had been a problem
that meant Elsa hadn't completed one of her tasks.
Once she had cleaned the old mirrors, I was embarrassed to see that when people spoke I gave little
smiles, my eyes rolled, I made a number of horrified
mouth shapes—everything ran across my face.

When Elsa talked, I would watch her lips and, if
she hesitated in her speech, suggest words. Often

I would tell her she was being unclear, that I didn't understand what she meant, to speak up. If asked by a customer about something Elsa had done, such as providing an armchair for them to sit in, I would deliberately misattribute the good results to the invigorating blast of fresh air brought in by Annie Milk.

LIVABLE

Annie Milk hung around the shop, staying silent and guarded, trying to pass me the things I needed, like a child who felt that other people were bigger characters than she was, their thoughts more defined, their moods more inconstant.

I was trying to figure something out about her but I couldn't quite keep her in my head. She came across as half-asleep, unwilling to be fully present, but required our support. She never volunteered anecdotes. Sometimes, she wanted to go over conversations I had just had with customers through which she had stayed silent, to add her comments in retrospect. She seemed not yet to have learned that she existed, and that she was, like everyone, visible, and had a degree of power in the pharmacy.

One Friday morning, when it was only the two of us in the shop, I engaged her in a conversation about what she wanted. She told me that she had studied politics, but as a child her dream job had been to be an air hostess. She showed me how she would gesture if she were instructing a passenger, pointing to the emergency exits.

I tried to involve her in my dreams about the customers' lives, but had to push against any neutral or depressing suggestions on her part. She would suggest possibilities, and I approved only those that came in a telegraphed, crisp, convincing style. Characters entered rooms and introduced themselves. "I'm George," they said, "and this is my twin, Raoul." As I stacked the shelves, I condensed her turns of phrase. Rhythms had to be just so.

That day she didn't seem to be as reticent as usual. On the counter was a pyramid of sunglasses, sports style, wayfarers, cat-eye. I began arranging them on a plastic display as she handed them to me.

I asked her how she had gotten the role with Mr. Malone. She said that it was because of Mr. Funicular's round-robin emails. The way these emails worked was that Mr. Funicular's acquaintances would send in jokes, and he would broadcast them to his entire contact list, which included Mr. Malone.

The joke was about a man commuting through Vienna. Every day, he walked by Beethoven's grave. One day, as he passed, he heard the ninth symphony blaring out of the grave, played backwards. The commuter was confused. The next day, it was the eighth symphony backwards, emanating from the composer's grave. The next day, the seventh. More and more perplexed, the man continued to make the trip to and from work, stopping by the grave, until a week later he heard the first symphony trickling out from the composer's grave, backwards. The commuter tracked down a music scholar in the phone book, a man who claimed to be a descendant of Beethoven's nephew Karl and an expert on his oeuvre, told him what he had heard, and asked for an explanation. "It's nothing to worry about," the musicologist answered. "He's decomposing."

It was not the first time that Mr. Malone failed to find one of Mr. Funicular's jokes funny, said Annie, and apparently every time he read a joke he didn't like, he would go to the phone and dial her grandmother's number. Others that he had stumbled over, misunderstanding them or finding them indelicate, were about intergenerational conflict and aging.

On the last occasion, he had asked for Helen's advice about a change of direction he wanted to make in his life. Helen had given him her granddaughter's contact details. Annie's eyes narrowed as she told me this, then she paused as though her jaw had become heavier. She had been traveling at the time, but he tried her on her house phone, the phone at her hotel, her mobile phone. When she finally picked up, Helen was in the hospital and Mr. Malone raved about her grandmother's turn for the worse. He declared in a frenzy that if she agreed to work for him they would also completely redo the downstairs of Helen's house together, make it livable. She told me that this reaction was surprising, as he had a complicated relationship with her grandmother. Annie clarified that the reason Mr. Malone had called was that he wanted to go into politics. Helen had suggested that her granddaughter could help him prepare his mayoral run.

NO DECORATION, NOTHING
PERSONAL

I thought of myself as the kind of person who could talk down a terrorist, or pacify a flasher unzipping in the moonlight and wanting to chat.

As Mr. Malone moved from the back room to the public stage, he would take all the information he had gathered over the years in the pharmacy to help him. It was so obvious how he could go wrong that I was impatient to calm the situation down, to save him from error.

At noon the side door clicked and I listened to his

shoes head across the floor of the back room. I caught him there and asked him how he planned to handle the confidentiality we owed the customers for the stories they had told me, which I knew he had heard. He suggested I come to speak to him at home. He gave me impeccable directions and told me he would be back around five in the afternoon. When at lunch I sent him a message to say I would see him later, he didn't reply.

I arrived late; he opened the door and shaded his face from me. His eyes had a disorganized expression I felt I recognized: they looked taken aback, scared, shy. It was a look of intense engagement, a statement that had a question in it, or maybe all this was just the evening light curved backwards as he turned away from the sun, offering to make a pot of tea. I came down the three stone steps into the small hall, and he closed the door gently. He disappeared into the rest of the house through a passage behind a partition. The room had no decoration, nothing personal, no photographs of strict-looking characters standing in front of wrought-iron gates, or with prams on the beach, or behind a dog that was facing away from the camera, their feet roughly in the first position of ballet, their arms held aloft at their chests as though carrying another, more wriggling animal.

When Mr. Malone reappeared with an infusion, he began to ask me about my mother. I watched him spooning honey into his tea. I could feel the same tug as I had felt in our conversation about Helen Stole when I'd dissolved into incriminating confessions. This time, I tried to give him only a little and observe what not to say.

I said that she had loved looking after people in crisis, and that this was perhaps why, when I was younger, I had so many crises, getting into extreme situations to provoke a sympathetic reaction.

I told him that when she had become ill, she seemed to have altered, and acceptance had been the quality that she valued most. She became irritated at people who didn't accept things as she did, thinking of them as cruel, stupid, or a walking calamity. After I had summarized this, I realized that, through this simple work of construction, I felt better.

Mr. Malone nodded and said he understood. He said his mother thought he should accept her faults, that he should be all right with the emptying town, that the town shouldn't resent the changing world. But he could never accept people leaving.

I leaned back in my chair so that he would go on.

Before he started nursery school, before she took a job in the city, before she moved out there herself, he had written to his mother with his objections, he explained. He curled his body into a comfortable position in his chair, and when he settled he looked small, scrambling. As a child he had thought there was nothing uglier than his mother's handwriting. He thought there was no tongue more disgusting than her tongue, which had deep crevasses in it.

I experimented with how little I could let pass over my face.

After his father died, he hated Helen Stole, who was his mother's closest friend, not because of anything Helen Stole did, but because of how his mother was around her.

Once, on holiday, he and his mother had accompanied Helen Stole to a weeklong teachers' conference

in the south. While Helen Stole was at the conference, his mother would take him out to a bridge or
a nice square and just sit and stare into the distance,
thinking hard, for an hour at a time. He hadn't realized she would do this. He didn't remember ever
having picked up a book until that holiday, when he
took up reading out of desperate boredom. In the
evenings, his mother and Helen Stole would have
fun together, become forgetful, silly. At the end of
one day, as his mother and Helen Stole retrieved the
keys to their room in the hotel lobby, he had waited
in a high-backed chair facing away from them. They
left without him. His face became less animated as
he spoke.

The year before her death, his mother stopped
wearing her slippers and moved back into the house
where her family had grown up. She would gaze si-
lently at her son and his friends when they visited, giving the impression that she might seize any moment
to steal away and go upstairs. That last summer, he
read books in an almost superstitious way, as though
the harder and more technical the book, the more
likely his reading it would save her life. He seemed to

return. Unlike her, he told me, he had always wanted change.

But even as he told me this, I could see him worrying that he wouldn't be able to conduct a relationship with me in which he would not get total control, total loyalty, just as I feared I wouldn't be able to arrive early, take stock of the inventory, open the shop, serve the customers, deliver medicines in the evening, and ten hours in, if I was lucky, walk Mr. Malone's dog every day—that it simply wouldn't be manageable.

He seemed to be weighing how much my flaws could be restrained, whether I realized I had them. He might have been wondering if he might one day hear these stories he had recounted to explain himself to me—when he had treated me as though I were a continuation of himself, had felt warm and convivial, as if he had been drinking, or as if he'd been living in an unpunctuated sentence with no silences—used against him. To lose his hold on this family history would be particularly painful, because he seemed to have felt so skillful in telling it.

My own voice felt different now; I didn't want to

talk loudly. After he finished speaking, he seemed to expect me to leave, and I went to the door.

It was in the morning that I started to question how judicious I had been the day before, if I had been obviously egocentric, revealing, unwise.

TAKEN SOMEWHERE

All the surfaces shone. The customers saw themselves reflected, pushed back, challenged by the door, the sides of the shelves, the mirrored walls. Reflections piled up in the front windows, each moment captured in light and teetering forward, over and over. Nothing drew your gaze into it the way the landscape—which was sad and ugly in the winter—did outside.

I was also a reflective surface. I made myself beautiful, as part of my improved performance. When Elsa commented on my new appearance I flicked the compliment away with my hand, as though my loveliness were so evident it was better left unmentioned.

I didn't like her calling attention to the work of production behind the scenes.

With August, I had learned to look lively, respond immediately, have a quick joke to hand, and explain exactly what my thought process was, unless I knew it would create problems for me by offending him. Occasionally he brought me coffee, bashfully parodying my former role. I went along with it. I wasn't hurt anymore. I didn't mind again.

The town had fewer inhabitants in the winter, and when they sat down in the pharmacy armchair to talk we lent them blankets from the wardrobe on the second floor, which now served as August's political HQ. In the front of the shop, if a customer referred to a piece of information I didn't know about, I repeated what they had said in a certain slow, excited voice that suggested they had told me something amusing and rude. I would describe customers' experiences back to them. "He threw you to the sharks," I would say, giving them direction as to how to feel about a story they had told me. Or I would comment succinctly: "A hair-raising experience." I loved the idea that the right phrase could ease harm, the way an effigy of a beast might protect a town from illness. I was self-conscious yet tried to act in unexpected ways, with bursts of fluency that did not betray the effort behind them, like a dancer. I didn't seek originality, but mined a corpus of clichés and useful phrases that made me appear as someone who could react quickly, collaborate, and empower.

My work was like sleep—the less I thought about it, the better it went. If I could have slept and worked at the same time, I would have. As it was, I just worked. I asked questions just to get Elsa talking, and when she braked at the end of her answer she looked confused about how I had got her there. She told me she was observing Annie like a hawk. Elsa had gone to the market, put on her sunglasses, and watched the way Mr. Malone leaned on Annie's arm. She said that Annie told him the nicer things we said about him. They were visiting empty houses in nearby hamlets to see if they could be sold to rich people. As she spoke, I wanted to close my eyes and rest my head on her chest.

At home I maintained a distance from art and books, and avoided any music that would lift or alter my spirits, which I preferred to keep as still as possible.

In the new year, August announced his candidacy for mayor, sending the required list of his supporters to the town hall. I told everyone who asked that I wasn't interested in politics and that I just wanted to hear about their lives. I changed the subject and said it was important to look after their feet. I asked them to show me their blisters. I had noticed that politics could become an opportunity for them to tune in to another frequency, and stop paying attention to how they were feeling. Everyone liked to be taken somewhere. Everyone liked to dream. I recognized all the symptoms.

But I responded with encouragement when August began sending carefully written mass campaign emails with grand shifts in register, abrupt cliffhangers, and anecdotes of people who had died. I submitted a glittering account of my time working at the pharmacy for him to send out. I recounted how easy he had made my job. I was marveling with a sentimentality that was really a feeling that I could teach the readers something I didn't myself believe. I felt my easiest way to being right, the charm, was recommending his work.

When I was talking to someone, I could sometimes feel Annie watching. Her eyes seemed to leap onto me, catch me and grip me. But if I turned to look at her, she never looked back. As August's candidacy picked up pace, he called Annie to the second floor more often. Annie bristled and seemed to make use of every second, every meter on the journey along the forest-green corridor and up the stairs to eclipse herself. One Tuesday she smashed a hole in a liqueur bottle's shoulder when she was fiddling in the kitchen and not wearing her glasses, so that August had to throw three dishcloths on the floor. I sympathized enormously and yet I was disgusted by her. "How many of these helpful gestures is he doing to save her from failure?" Elsa wondered, coming over to me in a gloomy mood. When the gossip about Annie's drinking reached me, I told Annie I never wanted to hear such embarrassing accounts again.

I watched as August asked her to explain a strategy, how under observation she hid her lips. They would develop canvassing routes on a piece of film they tacked on the wall. Sometimes there would be a tightening sound, the plastic skin shifting; in the morning the film would be on the floor. Was it the cold? Tremors in the walls?

Soon there were eggshells on the paving stones of the old town, crumbling like the green paint on its cracked doors. The sky was silvering. It was the start of spring. Far from everything and at peace, I felt as though I were tempting fate, that something terrible must be happening somewhere in the world, someone I loved committing suicide, a nuclear bomb. Along the streets where I delivered my prescriptions, bushes lined up conspiratorially. It seemed that I must be walking around in a long pause, an ellipsis, ignorant of a world event, as unreachable as the beast. Surely I would hear bystander reports of the catastrophe on the news hours later, when I got home. But I turned on my radio every night, and I never did.

Bluebells embalmed the woods and my daily routine felt like an extension of my dreams. Like rumors, the customers continued to circulate. They came to be saved from a symptom that was haunting them. They would look unsure whether we really could help. They didn't seem to believe that behind the counter there really was the syrup that would clear his head of melancholy or the pill that had been invented so that she could continue her life as it was without having to think of parenthood—that they really were a reliable witness to their bodies, and that they deserved to avoid pain.

PINCH, SKEWER, CARESS

One morning there was a stage in front of the pharmacy. At lunch an umbrella was resting on it. By evening, a microphone had joined the umbrella. Someone arrived with speakers.

A crowd gathered. August sat on a chair on the stage. The crowd shot him questions. By the time I finished for the day the square was rammed, and I had to stand in the side alley by the back room, down which August had once watched the stray dog disappear. I observed him from behind, laughing loudly at his jokes, clapping. Elsa laid some flowers to the side of his chair and a few minutes later the accountant rearranged them. August became controlled and soft-voiced, so that you could hear rivulets of emotion as he explained how the town's empty houses pertained to a larger loss of pride, twisting his torso as he went along, using his hand as a pinch, as a skewer, as a caress. He said someone had to take charge of the situation, which was why he had been holding discussions with developers. I had never heard him speak like this: there was a stirred feeling. And soon he was warmer than before, and some of his guard fell away. He moved his shoulders along with his arms. He used language thoughtlessly, like a gesture. He began to liberate applause from the audience, mentioning that he had been spurred to run by listening to the meaningful ambitions of his customers. The sun was starting to set, and light was hanging in the sheets drying on the balconies around the square. August bent his head back as if away from a spotlight. With one hand he seemed to be conducting the crowd, while the other encircled the microphone. Rain wrinkled the flagstones, and the accountant opened the umbrella over his head.

One more question, August said to the crowd.

He was pleading to stay in this new role, talking and twisting. He rearranged his chair, shifting his weight onto his feet, and in one movement, a swoop like a crashing wave, he lifted the chair off the stage and sat himself back down, still holding his microphone. The next thing we knew, he was on the ground.

That moment he fell off the stage was the moment I realized his chances of winning were really serious. Though his perfection had been threatened, the audience laughed at the collapse indulgently, as though he were putting on an entertaining character for them. Applause was ringing out as I left the square. What, I wondered, is the point in being a person if you don't inspire other people?

I SWITCHED OFF

Mornings were spent in the second-floor room writing up reports of his successes and afternoons sending them off in their hundreds. Downstairs in the shop, I secured credit so everyone assumed that if some woman had been healed, August had done it, and that if an important idea had been had, it had originated with him.

Increasingly I felt late to something, a meeting I couldn't remember or a drink I hadn't arranged. It was that dangerous time in spring: full of possibility but without direction. I was distracted. I'd notice just in time that I had buttoned my shirt up wrong, so that it clasped at my throat, leaving a mistake floating openly underneath, or that I had made an appointment and suggested a date in the wrong week.

The day Annie was late coming into the pharmacy, I was so tired that my face felt leaden and I could see in the mirrors that I had stopped emitting any interest in conversation. My eyes were closing. I had a cold that forced me to look at people intensely as I breathed in, head angled forward, direct. I reacted churlishly to children shouting and crying. I groaned and rasped and yelped and wept to myself. I had become strict, inconsistent. I was reading the paper and hunkering down, going to great lengths to avoid talking, leaving gaps between sentences that were too big, never picking up the pharmacy phone, and had decided I would go home early without delivering the prescriptions. I was trying to work out whether I should look at my glands closer up when Annie said she'd come in to say goodbye. She said she was leaving the town. "Why?" I finally asked.

Annie paused. When she spoke, her voice shook and tightened into a higher pitch, as if it were on fast-forward. "It's just time to go home," she replied.

I apologized for prying. I couldn't dwell on any difficult feeling. It was as though I had been staying as a guest in someone else's house and just wanted to cook something for myself to feel in control again, or had been sitting in front of an ancient, mysterious artwork over a long day and needed to go to the gift shop to exchange currency immediately. I was impatient for things to be done and to find out what happened next.

Elsa came into the shop and Annie added something about not wanting to fall behind her cohort by working in such a small place. She spoke urgently, chaotically. She seemed painfully aware that she wasn't sure of the exact shape or circumference of the subject she was dealing with. Elsa took an interest in this new side of her and they talked at each other for a minute before Annie left the shop. As for me, I wrapped Annie's story up with an easy conclusion. It was a shame but, after all, we had all lost parts of our own lives so that August could go bashing away at his new one.

I barely slept that night. When I did, I had a dream about a rabbit that appeared at a series of house calls

I made. The rabbit was being thrown from person to person, and everywhere I went, it was there too. Over the night, it became mangy and bloodied, and panels of fur came off. I remember someone throwing it in my direction near the end of the dream, its body paralyzed in fear, its claws out for gripping. Then I was forced to throw it off me.

TERRACES AND VIEWS

After I took over more of Annie's campaign duties, it became obvious that August had been making absurd blunders in his conversations with townspeople and the local press. He was exaggerating out of laziness, being too self-conscious, joking about who was sitting on the best chair. He was asked whether a neighbor would agree to a territorial change or who would buy the largest empty houses, questions to which he had no way of knowing the answer, but he couldn't help himself from volunteering a guess, so that he often made mistakes that would need to be smoothed over with long, street-like sentences sent by email.

He directed my writing to a bizarre degree, leveraging his understanding of the town's inhabitants. Mr. Paul, who runs the pottery, is an artist, he would say, not much of a thinker. He sleeps badly. Send him a message in the middle of the night to capture his attention. Mrs. Turner is beautiful inside and out. She won't need much pushing, but you must respond to her immediately. Helen Stole's memory is poor, and she is scared of forgetting. Leave that one to me.

He dictated; I began to type. "As long as action is taken to prevent the crumbling of our buildings and the wasting of our land, we will be able to turn the fate of the town around," I wrote. I learned never to add a period at the end of my messages, but to leave them open, giving them a feeling of rushing anticipation. Townspeople sent in testimonies advertising their confidence in Mr. Malone, and I transmitted them by email to all the clients the pharmacy had on record after improving the contributions, moving the paragraphs around, drawing out some of the narrative elements, adding a setting, repeating names, turning phrases so the weightiest word was stressed at the end of a sentence.

Elsa sent me photos she had taken of the

headquarters to attach. Typically she sent me the worst pictures. Behind three large wood tables pushed together on the second floor, August spread his broad palms on the desk. By his side, my face was straining to mirror his. It was peculiar that I didn't look at all angry. What kind of emotion was that? I wondered. My body language was awkward and stiff. Light streamed in through the tall, piano nobile windows.

As the campaign wore on, I noticed myself fitting around August, anticipating where he needed help, and saw him losing the understanding of what needed to be done to keep him propelling forward, for his mystique to continue mounting. Maybe he did at least comprehend the possibility of taking a supportive role, of being my mentor, but he wasn't actually able to fulfill it. Whatever it required, he couldn't manage.

Through my attention, I had turned him into a monster, hopelessly selfish, vanishing, ungrateful. He told me about that day's accomplishments and how they meant he wouldn't be able to do this or that, asking if I would do it for him. He pulled out a tangle of keys and a map, and showed me the rows of empty houses that I should inspect to see if they could be repurposed, arranging a route according to the connections he wanted me to make for him on the way. When I heaved open their old front doors, sheets hung where they had been thrown over tables and fireguards. The thick walls and wood features made me want to choke. Shutters and doors held the sun at bay, closing off terraces and views.

In the bar at the top of the town, I debriefed him about the houses' potential. Mr. Malone told me that this was where a famous poisoner had stayed the night, a man on the run from the forces of the law. Legend had it he had left behind a great quantity of vipers, and the room had not been let since. This confirmed my impression that the bar was a cursed place, where nothing good could happen. It had a long, bobbled entrance that seemed to be the piece left over from the entrance to the building next door. There were little cards on the walls—cab companies, restaurants, pet services. The room looked like it had chosen to ignore a lot over the years. Chairs turned away from the door and toward each other. Floors were heavily carpeted in a dated, durable weave. People with noncommittal expressions hung behind the bar, their eyes averted.

I shuddered, but he didn't notice. We played at having fun together, never really communicating. "Everything I do is for you," I imagined saying as I bit down on dry crackers and listened to the latest gossip about his friend's first boss, Andrew, or his neighbor's business partner, Jeet. "I've had enough," I was yelling, probably crying. But even in my head he just nodded.

Back home, I looked up the poisoner and found that he had stayed in another bar, which had since closed down. But it didn't seem to matter. I relied on Mr. Malone to provide me with stories—the great sustained surprises that would stun me away from life while reminding me of small aspects of it, a sliver at a time.

In the shop, I was still using his old techniques, using the word "intrigued" as often as possible, asking for elaboration, being prompt. Increasingly, I managed to control that mute feeling I gave off, my aura of uncertainty. All feelings would pass if I didn't engage with them. I have a weak spot, I had taken to telling people, a magic phrase that I used to trick my way out of an emotional hole, glossing over my blues. It's this or this or this . . . And I'd be really disciplined all the time.

FIRST LANGUAGE

In May, when we were in the square giving August a standing ovation, Elsa put her hand on the back of my hair. At first I barely noticed that what she had done was strange. Then I thought, who does that? She wanted to tell me something. She took a step forward and looked along over her shoulder at me. Her face was a heart, an apricot. It was the Thursday before the election, and lines of chairs were now permanently laid outside the pharmacy. The sky was slate gray, the light golden. I tried to signal to Elsa to wait but she was already leaving. For once her movements seemed to come from herself, not as a response to me.

I ran after her and caught up outside her front door. Someone was practicing the piano in an upstairs room of a house.

Elsa looked as though she had changed her mind about talking and would rather have given me the slip. She scratched her tense forehead. She told me August had asked her to check the messages I was sending to his campaign supporters to see if I was throwing my weight around. As I talked to her it began to feel as though a shell were descending over us, closing us off from the world. She said he had asked her to move some money from the pharmacy account to his campaign. Repeating what he had said, she looked breathless and hot.

She told me I probably couldn't trust August. She had begun lying when he asked her questions, and I should try lying to him too. She thought it was sad that I was feeling and worrying so intently on his behalf. I should revert to my bright, breezy email tone with him and keep my impressions of my customers in a notebook, rather than funneling them into the pharmacy laptop.

Elsa was right. There were no walls in my life.

Tomorrow, I told myself, no extra work on the campaign, just pharmacy.

The next day that decision felt like a betrayal, and I went straight to the headquarters on the second floor. I wanted to stop myself going, but feared that if I didn't, all my supports—the narrow house to live in, my finely stratified day-to-day, the glass of water by the bed—would fall away.

But that day was a local holiday and the office was empty. I called up the second flight of stairs but no one replied. Elsa convinced me to take a road trip instead, borrowing Mr. Funicular's small red car. Even as we had walked toward it, I had a feeling we could be entering a nightmarish situation, that having fun or letting go of August could only produce a dangerous outcome, one way or another. I was convinced I had left some open notebook in a compromising spot, but when I looked, my notebooks were all still in my rucksack. I took them out, shook them, and put them in a different compartment of the bag so that they were more enclosed and less likely to reveal themselves.

We drove around roundabouts, parking in all the villages, whose names were Cut-Throat, Escrow,

Relief. I wedged myself into the passenger seat planning our route as we went, and Elsa was driving, texting, smoking a cigarette, turning over her shoulder, asking me why I wasn't smoking.

We decided to visit a nearby cave and a regional art museum. Elsa asked for two tickets to the cave tour, and the teller gave her the price. We went to wait down some steps in a wide bowl of rocks near the cave entrance and started to argue about politics. She kept saying to me, "There's something weird going on." There was "a brooding feeling." She complained that it seemed like I didn't think things were as strange as she did. This was how she often felt.

"I don't understand what you mean," I insisted. "You're being vague."

Elsa was offended. "You're just trying to disagree with me," she said.

She told me she could see her sister's garden from her upstairs toilet. She had been looking down at it that morning and had seen her sister shouting at the gardener, a refugee. He had been shuddering with anger, perhaps because he wasn't speaking his first language. There was something going on, she insisted.

I suggested she block up the window that looked into her sister's garden, so that she stopped desiring it so much. I pointed out that her eyes fluttered into the back of her head when she was irritated.

There were now about fifteen people in the bowl. A tour guide climbed onto the wall. She delivered an introduction and handed out audio headsets. The cave visit took forty minutes. The walkway started down some steps. Lower, we would have to beware of the ceiling and walk single-file, avoiding the underground lake next to the trail. We wouldn't be able to see its glassy surface throughout, as most of the path was dark, but we should know that the lake ran the length of the cave. I pictured the tense position my neck would be in, the limits to my sight, the guesswork involved in putting one foot in front of the other. I saw myself holding my audio guide to the side of my face as someone pushed me over the railing, and going over, still pressing the voice to my ear. I felt the cold. I had a sickening feeling. Another woman and I realized we couldn't tolerate it, so Elsa entered the cave without me.

Later, when she found me in the car, I told Elsa

that I had also panicked in a previous cave I had visited, and that I should have remembered this before agreeing to the trip. I was afraid of small spaces, blood, speed, heights, danger, humiliation, and abandonment. The other lady, who was Czech, had told me that she had known she was claustrophobic too, but had thought she could overcome it on this holiday. I told Elsa that the Czech woman had communicated well, an ability that, as we rose out of the bowl together, she had begun to disavow. It was as though in her fear she had briefly forgotten that she didn't speak the language.

I told Elsa again that it had been the cave, not our argument, that had made the panic rise up in me earlier. She nodded. But she said she was worried I didn't want to be friends with her since taking over the pharmacy. I kept saying final things starting with "you always," pointing out her inconsistencies, and she'd had a dream about us being attacked from all sides, barricaded in a little house. I remembered that she had recently sent me an email in the night, in those minutes when the harshest part of the dawn chorus wasn't yet subsiding and one particularly loud bird was inverting a tune. She had been worried about me, checking that I was all right. I told her that I had begun to listen to call-in radio shows all through the night to stop my mind from running on, hoping that the voices, in their rhythms of joke, laughter, and interruption, would seal me away. I disliked living alone. Elsa nodded again to confirm that she had heard.

We drove around some more, over the curving roads lined with trees, the hills that plunged one way and swerved the other.

And even I had to acknowledge that a few of the pieces in the local art museum suggested a strange turn in the air, like the chair wrapped in barbed wire and hung on the wall, the film of students storming the national broadcaster in defense of a right-wing politician, and the photograph of a man who was kneeling on the floor wearing a jacket covered in insignia with an older gentleman looking embarrassed, standing nearby.

That night I didn't tune in to my program. I dreamed of standing on the square, seeing an army coming into view on the next mountain, and knowing that despite its distance from us still there would be nowhere we could hope to hide.

FLOODED

I didn't tell August where I was going when Helen asked me to pick her up from the city that weekend. I rode past fields of bearded, bedraggled trees beginning to bud, past the other trains with their triangle headlights and high-up doors lingering on the track. On the blinds, squares of light expanded and diminished. I closed my eyes until the way the train braked let me know we were underground—noise rather than sound.

The city was hot. Hatches lay open along the pavement as though its foundations were breathing.

Helen and I sat at her shaded balcony table with its
oilcloth. Across the street, a woman was putting out
underwear to dry on the inside rim of a ceramic pot
and then turning the pot away from the public, back
toward her own rooms. Annie emerged inside and
Helen called her over. After a while, Helen suggested
that her granddaughter walk me around the city
while she took a nap before setting off.

Annie kept us to the backstreets. She said that on
her first day August Malone had offered to walk her
around the town just like this. She closed her eyes and
made spectacular gestures as she spoke, as if flooded
with the feeling of exposing herself.

He had told her that if he became mayor he would
rename the avenue that led up through the town after
his mother. "You can name all sorts of things," he told
her, "squares, streets, stars." He took her up to the
abbey and showed her the statues he would restore.
They sat in the choir stalls, in a high-ceilinged cham-
ber with dark wood benches. He told her how hard it
was to get anything done. He said not to talk to Elsa,
that she couldn't be trusted. That I was responsible

for her grandmother's hospitalization. He told her that she probably thought we were boring. I, in particular, was a snob.

Afterward, he invited her to the bar up there. He wanted her to meet a friend, a prominent townsperson who had helped enable his campaign. The friend, an accountant, looked confused when he saw her, and left. Mr. Malone spent the rest of the evening making dramatic confessions. "I killed my mother," he said.

The next day, at the pharmacy, she brought the mother up lightly, offering something Helen Stole had told her. "I heard your mother lived on the second floor of this building. Was it this room?" He gave her an extra smile as if something awful had happened and he wanted to coax her into reacting calmly. "Last night," he said, "you were very, very drunk." He told her that several people had commented on it at the bar, including the accountant friend, who he said had come back.

Because she was surprised by his response, she left work with him to ask what he had meant. It had looked like flirtation. Elsa had asked where she was going and told her she liked her skirt. Annie knew now that she should have told Elsa why she was going, what had happened. But Annie was beginning to doubt that she was a good judge of any situation and she avoided another misunderstanding.

He took her to visit some of the town's empty houses. In the kitchen of a man who had been in the rope business, a heavy smoker, he told her the same story about killing his mother. She had looked over at the yellowed doorframe for something to do with her eyes, then tried to walk out, but he'd held her arms back against the wall. In the morning, he provided a different memory for her to remember. He said the stars had been out over the avenue. The green of the trees had been overwhelming and sweet, dreamlike. They had gone for a wonderful walk, up and down, up and down. She thanked him.

Over the six months she was at the town, he frequently—though she couldn't say how frequently, it was a blur—told her distorted stories about himself, stories that sounded like threats and tried to make sense of his wild feelings. He always acted as though the conversations hadn't happened afterward. At first she was curious, and would even try to imagine traveling with him somewhere far away, a place full of new, alien mountains and flights of stone stairs, where she could pass off this abnormal state of affairs to herself and others as simply foreign and unfamiliar. Then somewhere along the line the present had fractured open. As she was explaining this part, she put her hands to her mouth and drew breath, drawing too much. None of this was behavior I would have noticed in myself but it was obvious on her.

We'd come to a standstill as she seemed to evacuate the account from her body, and we sat down on a bench. A woman approached, with a flowery cane, a manicure, and bright pink lipstick. She asked us to move along so she could sit down, too. Annie made to get up and give up her place, but the woman insisted there was enough room for all three of them. "I'm only little," she said. We sat for a moment in silence, the three of us, before she began asking us questions. "Where were you from?" she said. Annie answered only vaguely. When the woman found out I had come down from the town, she said her grandson had just graduated from the city university and gotten a job there. "Do you know him?" A friend of hers arrived.

She sat on my side of the bench so that the two ladies sandwiched us, and the woman with the cane told her friend excitedly about the coincidence with her grandson. They chatted from either end of the bench, they interrogated us, and, finally, they left.

Annie said in one breath that she knew it was paranoia but she hadn't trusted them, and these days she thought she recognized people everywhere she went. In her apartment in the evening, she thought she could hear Mr. Malone's footfalls running up the stairs and his loud shoes coming down the chimney. There he was again, a bald head on a train platform. She kept going over the time he had scolded her for running away from him across an icy street, something she couldn't remember happening, after a day of canvassing. She had put herself in danger of slipping, he said. Another cold night she had lost her keys, and he had told her that there was nothing he could do to help. Finally, when she had pleaded, he had opened up the pharmacy and she had slept in the room under the roof on the third floor. The next morning, at his headquarters, he had produced his large key ring out of a coat pocket, slid her own set off it, and placed it on the table in front of her. His face was blank, as if nothing had happened. She told him she wanted to leave the town. He changed the subject. As soon as he stepped out of the room she received an email, quick as a flash, stating that she had expressed enthusiasm about staying on, laying out an alternate reality. Remembering her manners and her grandmother's faith in him, she had waited for another six weeks. Over that time, while he talked, some of his sentences had felt so long that she had thought she'd die before they ended. She hated him! She'd wanted to be on the other end of the world when she saw him enter the pharmacy.

She rearranged her legs in front of the bench. She kept being told by people whom she barely knew that her spine was crooked in some way, or that she was walking slightly oddly, leaning to one side. The accusations were starting to weigh on her. Every day, she noticed someone she was close to was telling her she experienced her life wrongly. She felt she was living on extra time and had started shopping extravagantly and stopped paying her student loan.

Having watched August Malone manipulate people, as though he believed he was having a variety of fun no one else was having, she didn't like telling this story or want to pull anyone this way or that. She wrote down what made her angry and realized she was behaving like someone she hadn't thought she would ever understand. She would repeat her fragmented memories to herself in streams to remind herself that they had happened, or pretend to be on the phone on the way back from the city center so that she could empty herself of them before she even got home. It didn't seem like talking had resolved anything at all, and when Annie finished she looked more anxious than before.

Sometimes, she said, she fantasized about never speaking again.

ORANGE JUICE

I was sitting opposite Helen on the train, my foot on the ledge in a mirror image of hers, my knee against her knee. "Annie told you," Helen said, finally. I nodded. I had failed to help. I looked back on the altruistic person I had supposed myself to be and found her repetitive and moralistic.

I could see the departures board through the window of the lazing train. I thought about catching one to the sea. The sea in my mind was a shambolic place, so shaken up by a storm that it was chalky and light, like paint. I had five minutes.

When I was younger and I woke up early, I couldn't

go back to sleep unless I had a glass of orange juice, and then I would feel drowsy again, and I decided to get off and go to the station bar to order fresh juice before the train left. The station bar was a lawless place where I was served by a young guy with a long face who was trying to establish banter with his boss. On the occasions that the young guy got a response, it came in a rumbling, dismissive voice. He cut six oranges on the counter in front of me and ran each half into the machine one by one, pausing to make jokes when they occurred to him. When he finished, he reached for a large glass but I pointed at the small plastic cups and back at the platform to show that I was in a hurry, and he said, "Ah!" and started pouring the juice into one of these. But there was too much. He turned to ask his boss what to do with the excess, and was told to pour it into a second, then a third cup. He did all this carefully, slowly. The boss twinkled his eyes at me. Together, they insisted I drink the two spare cups in front of them before I could leave.

I ran onto the train as the whistle went. As we pulled out of the station we could tell through the houses that slipped by that the wind had come up. No trucks were on the roads, because they were in danger of catching the wind and tipping over like sails. We saw slanted people walking along the grass, trees gesticulating like conjurers, the wind throwing water off the river.

There was flooding farther on, forests whose extremities seemed to have been cut with a razor, detailed, multi-floored clouds, and, in the distance, a herd of mountains like another country, blue and aerial, in the foundations of the sky. As we slowed down near the bend by the station, a group of locals was standing behind someone who was perhaps Mr. Funicular, dredging up something unwieldy and inexplicable from the turbulent river, a broad shape held together with sticks that had been gathering slime deep underwater. Densely patterned leaves and plastics clung to it like crabs. I didn't see what it was for before we passed.

THE ELECTION

On the Monday of the election, to avoid the tentative, encompassing morning rain, Mr. Malone, the accountant, the gossipy market seller, and the historian all set up camp together in the dispensing area of the pharmacy, eating big foods from takeout boxes—steaks and potatoes from the hotel restaurant—and the historian started to smoke inside, expanding into my space as he got louder and more relaxed, leaning into the curtain that separated them from the shop, until I came back from voting in the town hall and finally asked them to relocate upstairs; and late that afternoon, when I was leaving the pharmacy for the day, they were still there, on the balcony off the second floor, raising a glass to Mr. Malone's victory, the Vs under their chins lit up, toasting that little man with the briefcase, the accountant that had brought the last mayor down.

DISCOUNT THE DAY

Still, that beautiful scent of spring is even better in the evening, when the blossoms, and the green, and the shape of the mountains are just out of view. I was walking to have a drink with Elsa, who was bringing Helen Stole. We were avoiding the celebrations. I was worn out, so shivery, and ready to discount the rest of the day. I was feeling that my life would be short, relative to the trees I passed that were two hundred years old or the buildings that were tired. This decorative stuff I didn't take seriously would outlive me. I felt that I had been here before, and had always somehow known, looking forward, that I had just under a year in the town. After that there was a blackout, and nothing would be possible again in the same way. This was a certainty that had arrived a while ago already, and lodged itself in my mind.

I rustled down the street in my anorak, digging into pavements black as coffee grounds, saturated with earth and rain. At the crossroads, I could see goats making their way down the steep slope onto the path, sometimes carefully, sometimes jumping, as if they prided themselves on being indestructible, not holding on to one another, diminished, gray-skinned, gaunt, co-dependent.

When I arrived at the bar by the town gate, I saw that for the first time, the lantern was on. Elsa and Helen Stole sat outside with some wine. Helen kissed my cheeks as if she were eating me. Elsa wanted to talk about the rallies for Mr. Malone. "I found myself shouting things I didn't really mean," she said. "August Malone for mayor." Did she really think he should be mayor? Now he would be. As Elsa spoke, Helen Stole nodded, opened and closed her mouth in silent collaboration, pursed her lips, shook her head. I realized that I tended to think I was better than I was, and Elsa always thought she was worse. Helen Stole suggested that perhaps, having spent so long working alone with me in the pharmacy, Elsa was particularly susceptible to the pull of the crowd.

A moth fell from one candle to another. In the distance we could hear singing and, from the blaring municipal speakers, a backup of electric guitars. Helen was sewing, fixing one small spot on her shawl.

Elsa's voice was husky. She slurped her wine and ate the olives fast. What was mystifying about Mr. Malone, Elsa said, was how he stayed supported by the world. If he wasn't any good, then why was he winning elections? Why was his behavior confirmed by the people around him? She disheveled herself, tugged at her hair. She was sharp, quick, theatrical. She talked of ten-year plans. She couldn't sleep. Her house was spotless.

She kept the bottle near her. She spoke with such uncertainty about whether she would be understood that she gave me confidence to articulate feelings that I wasn't sure were common experiences either. I told them about the haunted atmosphere in the bar at the top of the town. It had reminded me of the apartment

I had lived in while at university, where I had received the call about my mother's accident, and after that had problem after problem. When we had moved out early, the student who took it set up mousetraps everywhere, putting off any potential further roommates. So we continued to pay rent on the other rooms. Helen was an articulate listener, carefully continuing our half-formed sentences, giving them body. Talking to her, you felt like a skeletal tree was being sketched faintly around your thoughts, a framework of branches that put them in a broader perspective.

She told me that her mother was given a plot of land after the war as compensation for her father's death. A wise man had told her that the land would bring the family bad luck, and indeed the uncle who moved there had had financial difficulties. When the family left, however, their luck turned, at least a bit. I said that I thought that maybe, come to think of it, all this had something to do with being able to take that step of letting go, that this in itself was a good sign. She said yes, that holding on to something when it's stopped being good, because you think it could be good again, is like gambling. Human beings pick up on much more than we allow ourselves to register, and those millions of neglected messages amount to a kind of intuition that is often right.

It was a conversation of agreement, guesses about the water we were all swimming in. I didn't find myself drawing back from talking about something unsafe, or that I might get wrong.

Helen said that she had seen August work for years, bringing in new people. He made sure only those ones who turned a blind eye were favored, promoted. I could tell that what we had said about him would sound much harsher in the morning, and that I would worry we had been hyping each other up.

Helen held up her work to the light like an astronomer peering into a telescope. "I think I need a thinner needle."

ODD, DEEP

The national press came up to the town to interview Mr. Malone. I heard from Elsa that it was all going well until he refused to respond to a particular question about depopulation, and when the journalist explained why it was important, interrupted with his answer. He rose onto the balls of his feet when he emphasized words like "what" and "go." As soon as he got the group excited, he would talk over their queries, as though he didn't need their interest, or was criticizing it, preferring discomfort. He gave the impression that he had read their minds, had preempted their most useful thoughts, and was guiding them away from mistakes. Then he shared his opinion on trivial matters, wrapping the proceedings up.

He wandered off in a dreamy state of relaxation afterward, and walked right into the pharmacy as though he could sense he needed to patrol the area, that ideas were occurring in there, coming together, forming outside of his control. He came to the counter and touched me awkwardly with an enormous gentle finger. "What are you talking about?" he asked me, and disappeared down the corridor, as though he sensed it had something to do with Helen Stole. He seemed a bit scared of me and I enjoyed that. I had an urge to fray his nerves. He came back into the front, yawning, and I heard his throat clack open and closed. He told me that he had suggested to Mr. Funicular that his amateur dramatics society put on a play to bring the town together. He yawned again. He seemed to be constantly pre, mid, or in the aftermath of a yawn. It felt like he was trying to distract us. I imagined giving a speech to introduce the play—but of course no one would ask me to give a speech. It was too much of a risk and no one had thought of it anyway. I suddenly realized that Mr. Malone's happiness had transported him into another decade and he was wearing flared jeans.

Now that Mr. Malone worked in the town hall and all his papers had been moved out of the second floor, I asked his friend the gossipy market seller to change the locks of the pharmacy. The market seller looked like he just oiled the hinges before losing interest, so Elsa and I took on the job ourselves.

As we were replacing the center screw, Elsa disconnected from our conversation. She hesitated. "You know how I told you Mr. Malone would get me to read the emails you sent, and check them?" she said. The small words she used made her sound like she was begging for mercy. "He also got me to write his speech about distributing homes and land fairly, and said I could mention gardens." She showed me a new ring around her belt loop with a large iron key. "In exchange, he got me to set up a replacement for Annie Milk. He wanted a particular guy. He said that this guy's job will be to walk around, to see if anything is going on." She said she was sorry about it now, and I searched her voice for indifference. She had thought something underhanded had been happening with Annie.

I put my palm on Elsa's back and she loosened, and asked if I wanted to walk home via her garden. I didn't take my coat.

She led me down the track she had first told me about, out of the town. Ahead of us, the river was shimmering out. The sound of laughter came from behind a shoreline of trees. It had an unusual ring to it. Over the hedges, the heads of walkers tilted curiously as they took their evening strolls. On the grass on either side of the path, picnickers picnicked. The river was clear, and I could see it was shallow, with wheels, empty bottles, and cans held on the bed. In the middle distance, at the points where the current was less strong, it glowed, ghostlike, echoing the lightest parts of the sky. Bushes rested, spreading over the water. Long wooden straws reached out from the bank and touched its surface.

Raising her hip to a metal door, Elsa slid in the old key and turned it. I went around her through the gate, and followed the path, bordered by dense vegetables. Within a few steps, wild old potatoes, radishes, overgrown onions, monstrous carrots lay sunbathing along the verge. They looked so shameless and calm.

There was fruit on the trees and the daisies and the dandelions and clover were out. In a box, the garden's previous owner had grown cucumbers, and they lay stately on the earth, dark green specked with white constellations. Elsa had already disappeared in a cloud of shaking leaves, then reemerged bearing a pair of extendable shears.

Lying next to the earth, craving a cigarette I hadn't had in years, I could hear frogs singing, odd, deep. I noticed the absence of light pollution meant that the stars were appearing in a dome above me. I heard a horse snort in the hedge. And I was suddenly floodlit with sensation—the extent of my body, the folds of skin, the pebbles under me, my raised hairs.

WAIT TIMES

All our well-rehearsed techniques went out the window when Mr. Malone's new assistant arrived, young and boxy-hipped, with a few stern streaks of gray in his hair. "You must be tired, you're doing too much," Mr. Malone had told me, elegantly replacing a stack of bandages that had fallen down. He suggested that his assistant could take over behind the counter for a few hours to meet locals, while I packed medicines.

As far as I could tell, the assistant spent the morning boasting about his connections and talking about art, perching his opinions at the end of pointed lips. When he expressed himself, he had a habit of sounding as if he were summarizing a much more complex position, like a troubled bishop lifting a precious chalice onto an ordinary table. He gave the impression he would rather keep his feelings close to his chest, preserved in their most nuanced form, unmuddled by other people. Things were "mostly" or "largely" agreed on by this or that group of people. When I heard him working, I wanted to lie down, and then I was really hungry. As I loitered in the corridor, I got the idea that one of these days I would go up to the third floor, where Annie had stayed that night, to reclaim a space that I had believed was uninhabitable, possibly dangerous.

While my mood flagged, Elsa took over being cheerful. She had become the bigger, brighter character, while I was the see-through and shadows, the blues and greens and indigoes.

The accountant came into the shop, looking around expectantly. I smiled politely at him, and he loudly breathed in as if I were performing a show. As he exhaled, it was like a violent and solitary wind was blowing over me.

Elsa stepped in and introduced Mr. Malone's assistant. "This is Annie Milk's replacement," she said, and the accountant looked strange for a moment and mumbled a comment that sounded like "An improvement." Mr. Malone's assistant looked like he knew what he was referring to. By this point it was obvious we should give up on thinking of ourselves as very intelligent.

We showed the assistant out around lunchtime, and walked him to Mr. Malone's new office in the town hall. The abbey's saints were rising into the sky. Saint John dangled from a crane above trees, above houses, leaning, the greenish orange of your skin before a storm. Saint Justus carried his head between his hands, spinning weightlessly, his stone wings twenty meters high. One by one they were traveling down the mountain by funicular to be restored. The horizon was crenelated where trees had been sawn down to pay for Mr. Malone's promised building renovations. The firs weren't indigenous anyway, Mr. Malone had said.

The heat was back. I had started work later than normal, and at five I closed up the shop, drew down the shutters, and took my trousers off early. I walked around like that and mopped the floor in the dark.

From that day on, I began to lose interest in my work. I stopped using my methods and talking about my Achilles' heels. I would give customers long wait times for their prescriptions, ask them to come back later in the month. Mr. Malone asked to meet me, perhaps to reprimand me for my lapse in standards, but at the last minute I changed my plans. "Something's come up," I texted him, "and I think I'm going to do it." At night I was restless. I stayed up as if to have the last word on the day. I began to cook, layers of finely chopped garlic, onions, spices, crushed rice. I found excuses to get out of bed and go wandering. I would potter, turn things over in my house, take a few steps down the street.

MY UNCLE'S DOING

Dressed in my white coat as I dealt with the customers, I caught my reflection in a pharmacy mirror. I liked the way I looked—monstrous, substantial. "Looking forward to my cup of coffee," I mimicked in the mirror, when I had a moment to myself. "Who am I?" I made the customers guess when they came into the shop. I widened my eyes, then turned my head one way then the other dramatically. I curled my hand into a crescent and put it around my mouth, playing to the gallery. "Looking forward to my cup of coffee."

My emotions had taken a long time to move in. In

the evenings, Elsa and I fried flatbreads in butter, ate them with yogurt, and lying down as I digested, I told her everything I was angry about. Mr. Malone's descriptions of each person's character and place in the town, which I had accepted because they were convenient and beautiful, were full of holes. His accounts of reality were unhelpful.

I no longer felt I could control how I was seen by the customers, or represent myself as I would have liked to appear. I was not quick and savvy, didn't hold my own. People's impressions of me surprised me more and more. Shortly after I returned from picking Helen up in the city I seemed to have acquired a reputation for being difficult. Mr. Malone had stopped complimenting my appearance. I wasn't interested in adopting a pleading tone, denouncing his maneuverings, or vying for his sympathy. Instead, I decided to reply to the email from my uncle.

It had occurred to me that as a child I had the reputation in my family of being furious, unstable, and drunk—my uncle's doing. The family had always been very concerned that he didn't feel uncomfortable, or diminished, or hungry, and one night I had disagreed with him at dinner. As he tried to ridicule me, I didn't back down. My mother hissed at me that we would talk about it later, and my father angrily told me I couldn't be angry about everything and left the room. Ever since, my uncle retold the story again and again as the time I had too much to drink. I had found it strange, a year or so later, to meet a friend's older sister—midtwenties, furious. I knew as soon as I saw the look on her face not to say anything. My fear of being as angry as she was stuck with me.

At the end of the day, I took my phone in my hand and, without resisting, walked down the corridor, up the stairs, through the door on the landing, and up another flight to the third floor.

UNDER THE EAVES

The room on the third floor of the pharmacy had shutters of a particular green. The effect of the heat and cold over the years and the way the slats had been painted and repainted by a slightly shaky hand gave the coating an uneven texture, alternately thick and thin. The light filtered through in waves on the rudimentary wood shelves with their religious texts, the wooden statuettes on the marble fireplace, the table lamp with a frilled skirt for a shade. The floorboards were sanded but unvarnished, as in an attic, and balls of fine wood shavings clung to them. There was a table, a rocking chair, a large mirror, and a bed for two small people, with a boat-shaped frame and high ends made of cherry. Trussed up in its brown woolen cover, with a rounded pillowy head, a white starchy collar, and wooden feet, it looked like a businessman. It had been made in winter, and the blanket would be oppressive, so I dragged it off and slung it over the desk.

Lying on my side, I paid attention to the marks Annie had left on the room, some hairpins scattered on the mantelpiece along with a toothbrush and paste she had taken from downstairs. I saw that she had decorated with candles. A cloth had been placed over the shutter nearest the table to block the light from showing on the square. I tried to close my eyes and walk through the rooms of the empty houses I had visited, and eventually it put me to sleep.

I woke late in a dent of Saturday morning light. As the heat rose, the summer sun slanted through green rows of upturned vents and stirred like smoke in the dusty air. When I checked my email, there was already a message from my uncle accepting my invitation to visit the town. He said he would be with me in seven days. He was embarking on some errands in order to get his vehicle into a good condition before the journey.

I imagined him planning the trip on the map, driving along the roads in his nondescript car, putting his foot down on the pedal as he joined the highway, pausing at beauty spots, reading the informational signs and then starting up again and taking the scenic route, noticing as the landscape slowly transformed to something more distorted, more pockmarked, more rugged, feeling increasingly at home as the sun began to set. I saw him resting for the night at an inn, laying his napkin on his lap, then tucking it around his neck as he began to eat. I was curious to watch him reacting to this place he had first told me about from the safe distance of myth. Maybe I even meant to force some process of confession. I broke off my reverie to put on some socks and head downstairs to the dark pharmacy. I admired my quiet kingdom. The mop was standing in front of the door where I had left it. I reached for the shelves and took a vaporizing spray and a face cream, then headed back up the stairs, stopping in the kitchen to wash my face in the sink and moisturize. From the slit window on the back stairs between the floors, I could see little green efforts growing out of the stone façade of the house opposite, and a bush, an explosion of life, below the birds' nests under the eaves.

The nights and days I began to spend on the third floor had a porous quality. I moved the furniture around. I cooked on the hob in the pharmacy kitchen and mostly washed myself in the sink after discovering the shower on the second floor was giving off a smell of sulfur. When dark came, I returned home to pick up provisions. On Sunday, I unlatched the shutters behind the open windows so that they slowly swung or snapped around with the wind. I could now hear the topics of conversation on the square and on the balconies underneath me. Mr. Malone's new assistant, who had taken charge of new conservation projects. The scandal of Mr. Funicular, who had been caught wearing a dress in a nearby village. His play had been called off—it was too strange. Staging it was like squaring a circle. Looking toward the future, I felt everything I needed to say now was so far away—blurred, indistinct, gauzy—that I couldn't reach it.

When the week started, Elsa kept things moving

in the shop downstairs, while I lay on my back facing the ceiling. I could practically see her, oversharing strategically with customers, tired until she noticed another big ego entering the pharmacy, then briefly on fire, then tired again when she lost respect because the big ego failed to restrain its will to be the best, to possess and control. I imagined her talking over the customers and indulging their interest in celebrities, royals, and so on.

I was trying to work out how much I could offer my uncle—if a conversation would feel like too much, if a walk would feel like too much. I felt I had long been overly generous. Would I pretend I had to get back to work if I needed to? I knew that he took any resistance from me as a challenge to him. I sat in a square of sun on the floorboards as it stretched into a parallelogram, and felt the breeze. I was in a sort of cocoon. After the shop closed Elsa came up to me and asked gentle questions that pushed at what I thought, what I wanted. I liked the meals she brought, leftovers all served in one bowl—marrow, parsley, cheese, ham, couscous, nuts, and labneh pressed together in an uneven mixture.

Later in the evening I called Annie on the phone and we watched a film together, *Spellbound*, trying to synchronize our viewing to the second. After having been mostly alone for a few days, I thought my voice sounded amazing. I took a nocturnal walk around the town. The air was cool. Elsa couldn't sleep, I saw. Her window was yellow, soft with light and heat, the curtains undrawn. She was sitting at the table. I walked past and didn't knock. Near the funicular, a man was shouting into the empty street, a lonely, angry tirade. I stopped at my house to take a bath.

I ran the water through my hands, moving the heat along the tub, picturing different scenarios, other ways the last year might have gone. I imagined the stage on the square. Mr. Funicular was insisting on putting on his play. "Where are the Gregory Pecks, the Ingrid Bergmans?" he despaired, as Elsa and I disguised ourselves with costumes and makeup in the pharmacy. He was leading a warm-up, breathing deeply, drawing his hands in and out, inhaling as they widened, like a pair of bellows. We ascended the stage, inhabiting our characters, the orchestra facing us. I was carrying a lantern on a stick. Elsa was swinging incense. Somehow Mr. Malone turned up in the script. "I must admit that, as he has upset me, I may seize any occasion to annoy him," Mr. Funicular had explained. I spoke into a microphone and heard a voice that shaped itself in a way I couldn't have anticipated: collected, distant from me because my lines were not my own words. Behind us were assembled actors playing a chorus of people who had no intention of changing, who would die, who would like the audience to think of them as shaded, complex, delicate.

I got out of the bath and looked in the mirror. One of my eyelids had collapsed a little so that I was no longer symmetrical. Veins popped out of my marbled skin like highways on a map.

From the window I saw a slight transparency appearing out of the darkness of the sky. I imagined another scenario. Mr. Malone had died of natural causes. He wasn't eating well and his lifestyle had been bad, the market seller said. He was killing himself. "Poor Mr. Malone," he chastised us, when Elsa and I spoke ill of him after his death. "August apologized to Mr. Funicular," the accountant informed me, "about calling off the play." "You all have memories of August Malone," the historian noted at the funeral. "Mine jostle against each other."

It was dawn as I walked back to the pharmacy. The horizon was glowing, unattainable. There were more gaps in the trees now, and they flickered, then burst into flame as the sun rose and I moved through the square. There was always a chance a fire would break out, that a match struck by a passing surveyor to light his cigarette would catch the ground, and these woods would go. The newspapers were full of fires blazing in forests, photographs of halls of gray ash, every difference converted to sameness. If there was a fire, what wouldn't I save?

My uncle emailed on the Wednesday to say that his progress was good and that he was going to make his detour to a metropolis off to the east, as planned, to pick up a portrait of a family member and a crate of wine. While he was there he intended to try the regional specialties and stay the night in a hotel on the river. He would start driving again on Thursday afternoon after visiting the museum. It would take him another evening and therefore he would arrive on Saturday in the midmorning if he set off early. I pulled on my trousers, shelved my hair around my head using Annie's bobby pins, and went downstairs. I had disappeared, but I hadn't gone missing. I emerged here and there, just enough to signal that that there was no need to pay me any attention.

On Thursday my uncle texted me that he had left in good time, sounding jovial, relaxed, happy to have a reason to make the trip and happy that I, his favorite niece, would be available and open to carrying out some of his plans with him, which I took to mean a long walk to a high peak followed by a rustic meal. He had never texted me before, and he came across as eccentric and delicate. I felt how I did when I saw someone's handwriting for the first time—that they were profoundly singular and vulnerable. I was more hardened now, whereas he was a sort of victim, an emotionally naïve and pampered man with no concept of his own power, an oaf, an idiot. I went down the stairs to the kitchen, opened the cupboard, took out a mug, reached for the tea, and plucked out a bag.

When I woke up on Friday I felt some pain. Whenever I had any time off work, my body revolted—a migraine, usually—so that I could not relax. I went to close the shutters. Up here at the third-floor window, you could see storms coming from days off. I thought about how my uncle would easily move me around the area, and the thought brought the pain on again. Taking deep breaths seemed to make it worse. I picked up my phone to check my email but just held it in both hands, letting go of it slightly and at once grasping it tightly again, turning myself away from the light, trying to forget the gaps in the trees. I heard some bags falling to the floor in the hall and Elsa was in the doorway. "Are you okay?" she kept asking, as though my life were a complete mess.

"I'm fine," I said. "Look how comfortable I've made the room." I missed my family—the way I was talking reminded me of them.

As soon as Elsa left, I went down to the pharmacy to pick out a triptan and a pair of wax earplugs covered in cotton wool. I used the nasal spray at a display mirror and went upstairs. After an hour or so the pain, like a series of switchboards, flipped from on to off and a wave of reassurance pushed me back into sleep.

I dreamed that my uncle and I picked up Annie Milk in the city in his car. Annie and I asked to be dropped off at a bakery for breakfast. My uncle was resistant. "Why do you want to go there?" he asked repeatedly. "It's just bread."

But we insisted. "We heard it was nice," we said. He pointed out the window at a shop called Bonus. "You can get bread, the same white bread there. It's a good store, cheap." In my dream, for some reason, he had a slightly faltering voice. "We've decided," we said. He kept probing, saying there was just one type of bread on offer in the bakery, speaking with difficulty. I could only see the back of his head but I knew he was ill. I was signaling to Annie, unsure if she was talking back to him conversationally, or was at risk of being won over. Eventually Annie was final. "We're meeting friends, sir," she said. "At the bakery."

My uncle began making bones about whether he could drop us off in front of the bakery, or if he would have to stop the car at the beginning of the street, where there were, he mentioned, dozens of other restaurants.

I asked him for recommendations of things to do

in the city. He started on a long list, speaking method-
ically, not inviting or acknowledging our responses.
In the bakery we found ornate pastries, arrayed in
columns, richly lacquered in glaze.

I woke up late, with no pain. A reverential hush
had fallen over the town. In the golden morning I
imagined I had woken up in a palace, in the lap of
luxury. The hazy sun came into the powdered air
as usual, the light a curling, syrupy Marlboro with a
sweet, piny edge. My uncle's car was parked on the
square. It was Saturday.

SATURDAY

I came downstairs and hurried toward the hotel where my uncle would be staying. At the crossroads I passed Mr. Malone waiting on the path with the accountant, who was holding Mr. Malone's dog on a leash. In the lobby, through the yawning of his shirt everyone could see the long hairs on my uncle's stomach, but instinctively no one wanted him to feel bad for even a second, and we all said nothing. We didn't want to be suspicious or impolite.

I was relieved to hear that my uncle's plan was just for us to go for a drive. If only we could find a topic that we could discuss for hours, the right distraction,

I thought, as I climbed into the car and we began to wind upward. "I met your mayor," he told me. "We got on quite well." He had a reputation in my family for wording things carefully, and as he applied his sensitivity to analyzing Mr. Malone, I knew that my uncle didn't have many friends and it was rare for him to like people, and that I should introduce the two properly. It struck me again how suggestible he was, how unreflective.

The landscape was blunt and would drop off without warning. There was no parapet on the edge of the tarmac, which was level with the tops of the trees growing along the ravine. We hugged the cliff. The sediment sucked inward, emaciated over time, or bulged out in lumps, as though objects—people?—had been hidden in the rocks. My head was turning. The hundreds of kilometers he'd traveled had made my uncle restless, and he talked of his plan for the return, the loop around to the west, the route back to the capital via a different network of roads, the visits to hot springs and historic cities—stops after me on his journey. Eyes casing the horizon, I caught glimpses of myself in the side mirror, my maladjusted hat. The sky was dramatic and controlled, with rectangular slabs of cloud and rods of light striping down in diagonal lines. I opened the window and closed my eyes. I will go home, I told myself. After we get to the peak.

When the road ran out we stopped the car and took the last stretch on foot. My uncle bounded along without ever getting ahead, out of consideration for me. He asked me questions. "Why are you so evasive? I feel like I can't reach you. Why are you always hiding?" I felt I was going to fly into a rage but I was out of breath, and after a few steps rage seemed like just another way of escaping. As I climbed I paid attention to his ugliness: his bulbous, stippled nose and shapely mouth, the impression he gave of pallor, his eyes at half-mast, his large hands and feet, his hunched, ashamed posture, and, despite all this, his momentary resemblances to my mother. I pushed at my memory. When I had fallen out with my family it had interfered with my speech, I told him, wondering if it was what I thought he wanted to hear. At first I didn't want to talk, as though the connection between feeling and knowing what to say had been torn. For a long time I looked for crowds, people who could swallow me up. I could only see one side of him. The dimple by his mustache twitched, his features seemed to travel closer to the center of his face, and his eyes welled up.

At the peak, the air was clear. I could make out every detail I'd had to guess at in the mist. I wanted to hold on to them and not let go. I felt nostalgic for these mountains even as I looked at them, and remembered as a child trying to cling to the moment of waiting in the wings before a performance, the effort I had spent trying to trap it in amber, the multicolored pins in the corkboard keeping up the lists of cues.

Before I give something up, I go back to it once, knowing I will cut it off forever. As we drove down the winding road, the trip back to the town took longer than I recalled. The sun was setting through the station arches by the time we arrived at the turn. We paused, suspended, facing the tracks at dusk. I imagined leaving on a long light-filled train, the moon swinging leftward and then rightward outside the window as we twisted along, the colors on the fields when I woke up, the sea mutating and reconstructing itself.

There was a shaking noise in the distance like the start of rain.

We came into the town through the gate by the funicular. At the gentle slope outside the bar, I felt a sense of familiarity I could admit only because I was leaving.

It began to shower.

Having found a table in the hotel restaurant, my uncle wandered around, drinking. We ate and then he fell asleep in an armchair. I laid a blanket on him and walked out.

The sky far off crumpled.

Mr. Funicular was at the crossroads. A comfortable smile landed on his face when he saw me. We slowed down to chat. I asked about his play, and his mouth, still smiling, dropped into mock outrage. As he worked his way around what had happened, I felt like what he said was a thin cloth he held over what he meant, letting me see its shadow or its shape protruding. If I pushed at the veil, the mystery under the surface would poke out. We moved around in each other's eyes. I kept thinking I should pull away, but I got a lot of pleasure out of just looking him in the eyes.

Acknowledgments

I owe profound thanks to Diane Williams, Nikkitha Bakshani, Francesca Wade, and Max Harris for giving me their read of different parts and versions of this book; to James Vincent for his thoughts and for his love as it was written; my parents and sisters Jeanne and Suzanne; to everyone at Soft Skull/Catapult; to Michael Salu for his art; to Seren Adams for her faith, support, and hard work; and to my editor, Yuka Igarashi, for her trust and authority.

Mr. Funicular's descriptions of the beast are drawn from Henri Pourrat's *Histoire fidèle de la bête en Gévaudan*. Language from *Contes de la Luneira* and *Le trésor des contes* (compiled by Henri Gilbert and Henri Pourrat, respectively) grounds the landscape of this book, and I am grateful to Bonpapa and Bonne-Maman for finding these folktales for me.

© Sophie Davidson

LUCIE ELVEN has written for publications including the *London Review of Books*, *Granta*, and *NOON*. *The Weak Spot* is her first book. She lives in London.